"You're Going to Marry
My Daughter."

Brant stared at the older man in blank astonishment. He thought of the beautiful young woman he had met earlier and what her father was proposing to do to her.

"You really are a no-good son of a—"

J.C. held up his hand. "That's no way to talk to your future father-in-law."

"You can forget that," Brant said emphatically. "Now if you don't mind..."

"I do mind." J.C. studied him in silence. "You find my daughter so unattractive?"

"That isn't the point. I'm just not the marrying kind. I'm lousy husband material. If you want to hire me as her bodyguard, I'll take the job. But I have no intention of marrying. Not ever."

"Maybe you weren't listening, Malone," J.C. said in a firm, precise tone of voice. "You will marry Denice, the day after Thanksgiving. Count on it."

Dear Reader,

Welcome to Silhouette! Our goal is to give you hours of unbeatable reading pleasure, and we hope you'll enjoy each month's six new Silhouette Desires. These sensual, provocative love stories are both believable and compelling—sometimes they're poignant, sometimes humorous, but always enjoyable.

Indulge yourself. Experience all the passion and excitement of falling in love along with our heroine as she meets the irresistible man of her dreams and together they overcome all obstacles in the path to a happy ending.

If this is your first Desire, I hope it'll be the first of many. If you're already a Silhouette Desire reader, thanks for your support! Look for some of your favorite authors in the coming months: Stephanie James, Diana Palmer, Dixie Browning, Ann Major and Doreen Owens Malek, to name just a few.

Happy reading!

Isabel Swift
Senior Editor

SDRL-7/85

ANNETTE BROADRICK
Made in Heaven

Silhouette Desire

Published by Silhouette Books New York

America's Publisher of Contemporary Romance

SILHOUETTE BOOKS
300 East 42nd St., New York, N.Y. 10017

Copyright © 1987 by Annette Broadrick

ISBN: 0-373-05336-3

First Silhouette Books printing February 1987

All the characters in this book are fictitious. Any
resemblance to actual persons, living or dead, is
purely coincidental.

America's Publisher of Contemporary Romance

Printed in the U.S.A.

ANNETTE BROADRICK

lives on the shores of the Lake of the Ozarks in Missouri, where she spends her time doing what she loves most—reading and writing romantic fiction. "For twenty-five years I lived in various large cities, working as a legal secretary, a very high-stress occupation. I never thought I was capable of making a career change at this point in my life, but thanks to Silhouette I am now able to write full-time in the peaceful surroundings that have turned my life into a dream come true."

To the real-life Denice,
who has become a very special friend,
with my love.

One

———

Brant Malone sipped from the glass of Scotch he held in his hand and studied the man who sat in the thronelike chair across from him—the same man who owned the Scotch, the palatial home they were in and, it was rumored, a great many of the flourishing businesses in the Dallas-Fort Worth area.

Jefferson Calhoun Roberts in the flesh was even more imposing than the full-life portrait of him that hung in the lobby of the twenty-story office building he owned in downtown Dallas. More imposing and just as intimidating.

Not for the first time, Brant asked himself what the hell he was doing there. If anyone had told him earlier that day—when he'd flown into Dallas from Atlanta— that he would be sipping Scotch with the man who owned the company he was employed by, Brant would have told the person to crawl out of his bottle and sober up.

He'd never even seen J. C. Roberts before this evening, nor had he ever had the desire to remedy the situation.

J.C. disconcerted him by giving voice to Brant's thoughts.

"You're wondering why you're here," he said, putting an expensive cigar into his mouth and puffing pleasurably.

Brant had already taken a careful inventory of the room they occupied. A combination office and study, the room housed a collection of rare books, furniture and artifacts that his trained eye knew to be worth in the neighborhood of a hundred thousand dollars. The contents of only one room in Roberts's home was more money than Brant earned in three years.

"Yes, sir, I am." He let his eyes wander around the room, then back to the man who signed his paycheck. "We don't normally move in the same circles."

A rumble started in J.C.'s massive chest, and his heavy body began to shake. The jowls that framed a prominent nose and fleshy mouth jiggled, then lay still once more.

Brant had just witnessed a rare phenomenon—J. C. Roberts amused.

Brant Malone was employed by the Roberts Fidelity & Guaranty Company as an insurance investigator. During his five years of employment, there had been no reason to meet the founder of the business.

He could find no reason for the meeting now.

"I wanted to meet you," J.C. explained.

That was reason enough, Brant supposed. On more than one occasion he'd heard grumblings to the effect that Roberts firmly believed his initials stood for Jesus Christ. At least many of his edicts were handed down like pronouncements from on high.

"I was particularly impressed with the way you uncovered the fraud scam on the Zumwalt's Jewelry theft. It was a slick operation, and one that would have cost the company millions. You were dealing with some heavy professionals who had covered their tracks well." His eyelids slowly lowered until they half covered his eyes. "As I said, I was impressed with the way you handled it."

Brant was never comfortable with compliments. He wasn't used to them and didn't need them. He shrugged. "That's what I'm paid to do."

The older man picked up his double shot of Kentucky bourbon, downed the contents, then smacked his lips, obviously savoring the taste. "Not enough, boy, not enough."

Once again the man managed to disconcert Brant. He hadn't been referred to as a boy since his tenth birthday over twenty-five years ago. Secondly, he wasn't sure he knew what the man was referring to—not enough bourbon or not enough pay.

J.C. demonstrated his mind-reading abilities once more. "You aren't paid enough. I've been taking advantage of your extraordinary talents for much too long."

Brant stiffened. What was it about that statement that made him feel uneasy? Certainly not the words themselves. What talents was the man referring to?

"You'll see a sizable increase in your next paycheck. I'm doubling what you're presently making—with more increases to come."

Brant stared at him in disbelief. *He invited me here to his home for dinner to tell me that?*

Eerily echoing Brant's thoughts, J.C. said, "Of course that isn't the reason I invited you to dinner." He savored the heavy aroma of his cigar once again. "No, I invited you to dinner because I wanted to get to know you better." His deep-set, hooded eyes gazed out at Brant like twin laser beams. "I like your style."

Brant studied the man across from him in silence. He wasn't particularly enamored of J. C. Roberts's style.

Take the dinner invitation, for instance. It had come more as a royal command—not an invitation. Brant had been traveling for weeks, following leads and chasing clues from Dallas to Atlanta, from Miami to the Bahamas. It had been a rough assignment, and he had been glad to have it behind him.

When he had returned to Dallas he had looked forward to going home to his quiet town house, locking the door behind him and hibernating for a few days.

Being alone was a way of life for Brant. He'd been alone since shortly after his tenth birthday when his father was sent to prison for beating his wife, Brant's mother, to death.

Brant preferred to be alone.

So he'd been less than pleased when he'd arrived at the tiny cubicle laughingly labeled his office to find a note on his desk. He was to call the executive secretary to J. C. Roberts.

"Why can't he wait and read my damn report," he muttered in disgust. Not that he thought Jefferson Calhoun Roberts actually wasted his time on the internal functions of the business. Roberts Fidelity & Guaranty was only one of the pies he had his fingers into. But why else would Brant be expected to contact him?

He pushed a wave of black hair off his forehead with impatient fingers, reminded himself he needed to get a haircut and picked up the phone. He couldn't ignore the call. He liked his job, he liked the company, and he particularly liked Dallas, partly because it was nothing like the series of hellholes he'd lived in for fifteen years.

When the woman answered, he identified himself.

"Oh, yes, Mr. Malone. Mr. Roberts would like you to have dinner with him tonight." The carefully polished disembodied voice could easily have been mistaken for a talking computer for all the feeling that accompanied the message. "His car will pick you up at the main entrance of the building at five o'clock to drive you to his home."

"His home?" Brant repeated in disbelief. He knew of no one at the company who had been at Roberts's home. It was rumored to be as inaccessible as Fort Knox.

"That is correct, sir," the polite voice recited.

Well, that certainly shot down his plans for the evening—to go home, find a bottle of Scotch and nurse it through a few mindless hours of television. He wasn't sure he could live with the disappointment.

"Fine. I'll be there."

"Of course," came the smooth reply.

Good point. There had never been any doubt in anyone's mind that, if J. C. Roberts spoke, everyone listened—and obeyed.

The long, sleek black limousine with smoked glass windows had waited in isolated splendor in front of the building—in the No Parking zone. Several people glanced curiously at it when they came out of the building so that Brant felt somewhat conspicuous when he strode over to the uniformed driver who stood near the right rear door.

The driver gave him a quick once-over that made Brant feel he'd just been visually searched with X-ray vision. "Brant Malone?" he asked.

Brant nodded curtly. He wasn't feeling particularly loquacious at the moment. The five o'clock crowded confusion of downtown Dallas swirled and eddied around them. Traffic on the street was already bumper to bumper.

The driver opened the rear door and stepped back, allowing Brant to get in. The back seat could easily have seated five people without crowding, and two more rows could have fitted between Brant's luxuriously padded bench seat and the one in front. Glass separated them. *Naturally,* he decided. *One mustn't mingle with the staff.*

The driver climbed into the front seat and spoke through the intercom system. "If you pull down the folding table in front of you, sir, you will find the bar, if you'd care for a drink."

Now that was the best offer he'd had all day. Following instructions, Brant discovered an extremely well-stocked miniature bar, complete with ice, mixers and a small blender. All the comforts of home—and then some.

As he sat back and sipped on his very old, very expensive Scotch, Brant leisurely took in the scene before him. They were headed north on North Central Expressway.

As usual the traffic was enough to cause a person to dream of escaping to a tropical island somewhere where the sound of a horn and the squeal of tires and brakes had never been heard.

Now this is the only way to face North Central Expressway traffic during rush hour. He silently toasted his absent host and took a deep, reviving swallow of the excellent Scotch.

The limousine continued north through the suburbs of Richardson and Plano, and Brant began to wonder if Roberts's mysterious abode was even in Texas—they were less than an hour's drive from Red River, which separated Texas from Oklahoma.

Several miles north of Plano the limousine took one of several farm road exits that periodically decorated the interstate highway. This one looked no different than the last five they had passed. Obviously the driver knew something Brant didn't.

For the next several miles the limousine followed a secret route of its own. They made a left, a right, another right, then two lefts onto various country roads until Brant was convinced they would soon find themselves back at the interstate having gone in circles—or squares, as the case may be.

The last road they turned onto was marked Private, No Trespassing. Brant sat a little straighter and began to observe the passing scenery with more interest.

This part of Texas wasn't noted for its trees, but the lane they followed was lined with them. The early October weather had done nothing to disturb their thick foliage.

Brant noticed the driver speak into a small hand-held mike, but the glass between them effectively prevented eavesdropping. The car made a sharp right turn and stopped at a wrought-iron gate, the only opening in two towering brick walls that stretched away from the driveway toward infinity, or the state line, whichever came first.

The driver continued to speak into the hand-held set. Slowly and silently the gate parted before them, and they passed through.

Brant glanced back through the rear window and saw two men stationed just inside the gate, one on each side. One man stood in front of a small gatehouse. They watched expressionlessly while the limousine pulled away and gathered speed once more.

For a private residence, the security measures were awesome. Brant considered himself an expert in security measures. There had been times in his past when this skill was the only thing that had kept him alive.

Inside the brick walls the grounds reminded Brant of Southern California more than northern Texas, and he found himself wondering if J. C. Roberts had figured out a way to control the weather in order to produce the profusion of multicolored lushness that surrounded the area.

J.C.'s palace—and to consider it anything less would have been an insult—must have covered several acres of land. There were three stories in blinding white stucco and scarlet Spanish tile. The style reminded Brant of homes he'd seen scattered around the Mediterranean.

He wondered if all of the splendor he'd been suddenly exposed to was supposed to render him speechless.

He'd never considered himself much of a talker, anyway.

By the time the English butler ushered him into the study, Brant was convinced nothing else could faze him. His only moment of surprise came when his arrival wasn't announced with a trio of trumpets and two flag carriers. He supposed they had to skimp on something.

Now he sat in the study, wondering what was expected of him.

"Dinner is served."

Brant could have sworn the words, "your excellency," echoed in the air, the tone of the dinner announcement was so formal.

J.C. stood up for the first time since Brant had walked into the room. The expert tailoring of his suit did much to camouflage the fact that he needed to lose at least fifty pounds—perhaps seventy-five for today's health-conscious society.

He motioned Brant to follow the tall, stately figure of the butler across the entryway that was only slightly smaller than one of the air terminals at the DFW international airport.

The dining room and main table could have been used to seat the entire squad of the Dallas Cowboys with plenty of elbow room, and Brant was pleasantly surprised to be ushered past the seemingly mile-long table to an alcove of the room where a small one had been tastefully arranged. Spice-scented candles flickered, their color duplicated in several shades of the floral centerpiece. Tasteful and elegant.

J.C. had obviously invited the wrong person for dinner. This was definitely not Brant's scene.

He had just noticed that the table was set for three when he heard a light, feminine voice behind him.

"I'm sorry to be late, Father. I hope you'll forgive me."

Brant turned around and stared in disbelief. The young woman standing there was Roberts's daughter? Impossible. Utterly and totally impossible.

She was of average height, but that was the only thing average about her. Her russet-colored hair bounced and swayed around her shoulders as she moved, the candlelight reflecting glints of flame in the deep waves.

Her sherry-colored eyes, surrounded by long, thick lashes, glinted with amused good humor and just a hint of well-bred curiosity when she glanced at Brant. A connoisseur of perfect beauty might conceivably point out that her nose was slightly tilted at the end and her mouth was a little too wide for classic beauty, but Brant never noticed those slight imperfections. Her mouth was decorated with such a loving smile, it made him suddenly wish the smile had been directed at him.

"Ah, there you are, my sweet. Your timing, as usual, is impeccable." J.C. kissed the woman on the cheek and patted her shoulder in a clumsy caress. Taking her hand, he led her over to Brant, who was still unable to believe the evidence before his eyes.

"Darling, I want you to meet Brant Malone, one of my most valued employees and I hope trusted friend. Brant, may I present to you my daughter, Denice."

Her smile remained warm and her eyes sparkled as she looked up at him. She held out her hand. "I'm very pleased to meet you, Mr. Malone. You really *must* be special. Father seldom invites anyone to our home."

Brant automatically grasped her hand, its soft slenderness lost in his much larger grasp. The slight scent of a floral perfume reached him. It was as evocative and unusual as she was.

Brant searched for something to say. Usually he was never at a loss for words, but this was not a usual situation, not by a long shot.

"How do you do, Miss Roberts. I'm afraid you caught me by surprise. I wasn't aware Mr. Roberts had a daughter."

"Call me J.C., Brant," J.C. boomed. "I don't want to hear any of this mister business here in my home."

The butler pulled out a chair, and Denice sat down. J.C. and Brant took the other two chairs, so that they faced each other.

As though there had been no interruption, J.C. continued. "I don't broadcast the fact I have a daughter, Brant. A man in my position can't be too careful. I wouldn't want anything to happen to her. That's why I sent her back East to school." He glanced at his daughter. "How are things at the hospital, my dear? Busy as usual?"

"Same as always, Father. There were several admitted while I was away."

J.C. explained. "Denice is a trained physical therapist. She currently spends most of her time at the children's hospital. I managed to talk her into visiting back East with old college chums to relax for a few weeks. She just got home a couple of days ago."

"I'm sure Mr. Malone isn't interested in hearing about me," Denice said with a smile of apology. She gave a barely perceptible nod to the butler, signaling that dinner should be served.

Brant recognized the poise and polish of an exclusive finishing school, and yet the urbane sophistication didn't overpower a natural friendliness and warmth that seemed to radiate from her.

"How long have you worked for Father, Mr. Malone?"

"Five years. And the name is Brant."

A dimple suddenly appeared in her left cheek when her polished smile widened briefly into a gamine grin. "And mine is Denice."

The first course arrived, and there was a pause in conversation as though each party was regrouping, preparing for the next stage. Brant wished to hell he knew what was going on and why he was here. He had absolutely nothing in common with these two people.

"Are you originally from Texas, Brant?" she asked after a few minutes.

"No. I grew up in upstate New York." The lie fell easily from his lips, he'd repeated it so often.

"What brought you to Texas?"

"The lure of warmer winters. If I never see another snowstorm, I won't miss it." By God, that was certainly the truth!

She chuckled, a husky, warm sound that did strange things to Brant. Unfamiliar things. Brant didn't care for the unfamiliar, not anymore.

"I know what you mean. I thought it was because I was raised here in the Sunbelt and didn't grow up playing in the snow. For whatever reason, I have never cared for cold weather, either."

J.C. cleared his throat, then spoke. "What do you think of the Cowboys' chances of winning their game this week, Brant? Or aren't you a football fan?"

"I try to watch when I can, but my schedule doesn't always mesh with theirs. They're playing the Steelers, aren't they?"

"That's right." J.C. then went into an involved discourse regarding the two teams, their players and their coaches, evaluating each one carefully. Brant realized that J.C. took his football very seriously. His next words confirmed it.

"There's a great game scheduled for Thanksgiving, by the way. You're welcome to join us at the stadium, Brant. We have a box there."

Brant glanced at the woman who sat eating calmly as though the conversation between the two men had nothing to do with her.

"Well, I don't know if I'll be in town on Thanksgiving—"

"Nonsense. Where else would you be? Certainly not working. I'm not that much of a slave driver."

"Perhaps he intends to spend the holidays with his family, Father. That's not unheard of, you know."

Her eyes sparkled in the candlelight, and that mischievous dimple winked at him, then disappeared. "Does your family still live in New York, Brant?"

He carefully rested his fork on his plate and politely touched his mouth with his linen napkin. "I have no family."

His voice sounded more harsh than he intended. It was particularly noticeable immediately following Denice's lighter friendly tone.

"Oh."

For a brief instant he felt as though he had brutally slapped an inquisitive kitten, causing it to tumble backward in pained surprise.

He clenched his jaw, then deliberately picked up his fork and began to eat again.

Although Denice did a credible job of keeping the conversation moving, her sparkle seemed to have disappeared. And after dinner, when she suggested coffee in the study, she excused herself after one cup and left the men alone.

J.C. immediately poured each of them a healthy snifter of brandy and lit up another cigar.

"You were a mite harsh with Denice back there, don't you think?" he drawled lazily.

Brant swirled the liquid in the graceful container and watched the flame from the fireplace catch and reflect the glow. Denice's hair had seemed that same rich color—like brandy lit by firelight. He glanced up at the man watching him with hooded eyes.

"I never had many social graces." He took a sip of the aged brandy and rolled it around on his tongue, enjoying the bite, the heat and the smooth way it glided down his throat. There was something to be said about being able to afford the best that money can buy.

"She'll get over it," J.C. commented, staring into the fire.

The two men sat there, enjoying the peaceful sounds of the wood popping in the fireplace, watching the gold and blue flames dancing above the logs while the bright orange of the coals glowed below.

Brant found himself relaxing for the first time in weeks—possibly months. He was glad he had come. J. C. Roberts in the flesh was not as intimidating as he had first thought. Perhaps seeing him with his daughter had shown Brant another side of him. There was no doubt he loved her very much.

Brant could understand why. Denice seemed unaffected by the staggering amount of wealth that surrounded her. She appeared natural and unspoiled.

"I can't remember when I've enjoyed a more delicious meal," Brant finally roused himself enough to say. "My compliments to the chef."

J.C. waved his hand negligently. "I believe that you always get what you pay for. I pay for the best."

A commendable philosophy, Brant agreed silently, *if you can afford it.*

"What did you think of Denice?"

What did he think of Denice? Good question. Several rather complicated answers danced around in his head. She was out of his league, but he recognized intelligence, beauty and class when he was exposed to it.

"She's one hell of a woman," he heard himself murmur, surprised that he'd voiced that particular thought.

"Yes, she is," J.C. agreed emphatically. "She's her mother all over again. Thank God she didn't take after me." He smiled, amused by his own comment. "She's all I've got."

"You must be very proud of her."

"Oh, I am. Proud, but aware of the tremendous burden I've placed on her."

"How's that?"

"By creating this empire, then leaving her to run it."

Brant glanced at the older man, surprised at the somber tone. "I wouldn't worry about it, if I were you. You've got several more years of productivity ahead of you." Brant felt a little uneasy at the sudden turn in conversation. J.C. didn't strike him as the type to get maudlin after a few drinks. He checked the clock on the mantel and wondered whether he could suggest that he needed to go home without seeming to be impolite.

Brant glanced back at the older man and found him studying him intently. J.C.'s expression suddenly reminded Brant of a man he had known in Europe—a man totally without scruples, who let nothing stand in his way when he made up his mind about something. Brant became aware that the quiet, overweight, slightly inebriated host who had been sharing the peaceful firelit solitude with him was gone. The man now seated across the fireplace from him lived up to the public image of Jefferson Calhoun Roberts—a ruthless, ambitious, no-holds-barred builder of empires and fortunes. He looked dangerous.

Brant was so enmeshed in reconciling the metamorphosis that he didn't immediately absorb the meaning of the words J.C. spoke in a calm, quiet tone of voice.

"The doctor says I'll be lucky if I live to see the new year in."

The calm, dispassionate statement showed less emotion than he'd shown discussing the Cowboys' chances of going to the Super Bowl.

Brant stared at the man. He didn't know what to say. Instinctively Brant knew the reason for the dinner invitation had something to do with the quiet announcement he'd just heard. Questions, vague premonitions and unfinished statements buzzed in his head. They coalesced into one short, brutal question.

"Why are you telling me?"

J.C. allowed himself the luxury of a small smile. "I never make a mistake about a man. Never." He puffed on his cigar, then sipped on his brandy, a smug look of approval on his face.

"None of that stuff can be helping you any," Brant said in an irritated voice, nodding toward the brandy and cigar.

"We all have our own way of dying. Let me enjoy mine."

"Does Denice know?"

"As far as she is concerned, her father is indestructible, possibly immortal."

"Do you think you're being fair to her?"

"Fair? That's a strange word coming from you, Brant. You learned a long time ago that life isn't fair. You learned that early and well."

That was the second time that evening J.C. had alluded to Brant's background, the background that had been carefully hidden five years ago.

All of Brant's inner alarms were jangling, and with sudden certainty he realized he had been set up. He had been lured there by his curiosity, plied with fine liquor and haute cuisine, lulled by soothing conversation, and now securely pinned in the trap. He knew it—he sensed it—but he still couldn't see it. What was the trap? And why him?

Playing for time, he reached into the enameled holder on the table next to his chair and casually drew out a cigarette. Lighting it with the lighter that lay nearby, he ruefully noted that this was his first cigarette in three years. He had never needed one more.

Inhaling deeply, he leaned back in the chair and forced himself to relax. So he'd gotten caught with his pants down on this one. He hadn't even seen it coming. At least in his former line of work he had always known who the enemy had been—everyone he met.

It had been the only way to survive—and he had survived. *I've grown soft these past few years. Now I'm going to pay for it.* But damn! He wished he understood how.

"What do you want from me?"

A wolfish smile of satisfaction appeared on J.C.'s face. "Yes," he said, as though agreeing to an unheard remark, "you're a very smart man." His eyes were practically hidden behind his heavy lids. "How much do you know about me, Brant?"

He shrugged. "Not much. Several rumors and speculations. Why?"

"Because if you know anything about me, you'll know I always get what I go after. I never bluff. My business practices wouldn't always pass a close scrutiny, and I've made a few enemies over the years."

"Imagine that," Brant murmured, stretching out his legs and crossing them at the ankles.

"I've made damn sure Denice was protected from my business, something I neglected to do for her mother. I paid dearly for that mistake. Denice believes in the image I have always portrayed to her—that of a loving father. It was easy enough to do. Denice is damned easy to love, even if she is my daughter."

J.C. got up and poured himself another drink. Holding the bottle up in a silent question, he waited until Brant shook his head before placing it back on the bar and returning to his chair.

"I don't blame you. It's a good idea to keep a clear head." He chuckled at his own joke.

Sinking back in his chair once more, J. C. tasted the brandy and sighed with satisfaction. "Denice thinks we live in a fortress because I fear kidnappers. That's true enough. But there are some who are waiting for a chink in that wall out there, just one tiny toehold to help them get inside and take over.

"When I go, my empire is going to be swarmed unless I do something to stop it."

"And that's where I come in," Brant said with quiet certainty. He could feel the adrenaline start to flow. It had been years since he'd felt the sensation. It only came when he pitted himself against overwhelming odds. It was a high that couldn't be duplicated in any other way. And his reaction to its presence forced him to acknowledge his addiction.

Brant could feel his heart's rapid beat shaking his chest, could almost feel the blood racing through his veins. How did J. C. Roberts know he would be willing to tackle such a challenge?

"Why me?"

"I've been interested in you for some time, Brant. You fascinate me. You really do. Because you're a lot like me. You're ruthless about getting what you want and you don't let anyone lean on you."

"So what exactly do you have in mind for me to do? Be some sort of bodyguard to Denice? Oversee your empire? What?"

J.C. leaned back in his chair and laced his fingers over his considerable paunch. With his eyes almost closed, he deliberately drawled, "You're going to marry my daughter."

Two

———

Denice Roberts wandered restlessly through her suite of rooms. She wasn't sure why she couldn't settle down to either television or a book. After her recent traveling schedule, a quiet evening at home was just what she needed. But perhaps that was it. Her hectic schedule had wound her so tight she couldn't seem to unwind.

She didn't want to think that her restlessness had anything to do with her father's dinner guest. Denice forced herself to sit down and confront her reactions. If she had learned nothing else in her twenty-four years, she had learned to be honest with herself. She had come to know how painful honest reflection could be, but she refused to shy away from it.

So. There was something about Brant Malone that disturbed her. There. She'd admitted it. As a matter of fact, there were a great many things about the man that disturbed her.

His looks, for instance. It wasn't his height. She was used to tall men, although Brant was even a couple of inches taller than her six-foot father.

There was something about his face—a hardness, a lack of gaiety, as though he never smiled. His mouth went through the polite motions, but his eyes never changed. It was his eyes that disturbed her—black eyes without a glint of light in them—so black the pupils seemed to be part of the color.

His eyes gave nothing of his thoughts away. He was polite, uttering the proper social patter in a rough, deep timbre. His voice made her think of late-night or early-morning murmured conversations, a husky, rusty-sounding voice that was unused to speech.

His thick, black hair was a little too long for fashion, and he seemed unaware of how the slight wave that tended to fall across his forehead softened the austerity of his face.

His face fascinated her—high cheekbones and lean cheeks, a strong jawline, eyes that slanted slightly. A Slavic face, which was strange. She thought of Malone as an Irish name. Perhaps he had gotten his looks from his mother.

What sort of man was he? Who was he? Her father said he worked for him, but he didn't explain in what capacity. Executioner, perhaps?

Where had that gruesome thought come from? Perhaps it was the way he had dressed—all in black—that had given him a certain sinister appearance. His black silk shirt had told her he enjoyed expensive clothes. The black leather coat could have been designed with his physique in mind. His shoulders were wide and heavily muscled, and his body narrowed to a lean waist and long muscular legs, shown to advantage in his well-tailored black slacks. He looked lean and mean. And lonesome.

Once again, she wasn't sure where that thought had come from. A lonesome executioner? She laughed out loud at her silliness.

And yet—he certainly didn't strike her as the type of man she'd want for an enemy!

As a lover, perhaps?

She flung herself out of the chair and began to pace. All right! So he had a brooding, mysterious air about him that most women would find tantalizing. He moved like some wild jungle cat—silently, softly, relaxed but alert, so he could suddenly spring on the unwary.

If you cared for that type.

What type, exactly, attracted her? She didn't know. Denice tried to think back to the men she had known and for the first time in her life faced the fact that she didn't know very many.

Her father's fortune had seen to that.

From a very young age, Denice had always known her father was different. He had never allowed her to attend public schools and had seen that she'd never gone anywhere unescorted. Every young man she'd ever dated had been carefully scrutinized before he'd been given permission to date her.

No wonder not many came back.

She hadn't cared. Denice had never seen her father's rules as restrictive. She had known they were made from love—because he feared for her safety.

For good reason. Her mother had been killed by a hit-and-run motorist when Denice was five years old. The driver had never been identified. She grew up knowing she was all her father had. Even as a young child she had understood his grief and anger.

What she realized was that she had never known a man even remotely like Brant Malone. She wasn't sure that she wanted to.

Denice was content with her life. She loved children, and with her training she had found an opportunity to be around those she could help. Sometimes she took special cases—those children nobody could seem to reach.

In addition to her special training, she gave them something else—her love. She gave it freely, unconditionally, expecting nothing in return. Some of them were suspicious of her motives and waited for the catch. Once they came to know her they finally discovered the truth: there was no catch.

She had caught a glimpse of something tonight in Brant Malone's eyes that reminded her of some of her tougher cases. A sort of incredulity, as though he were asking "Are you for real?" She had sensed his defensiveness, a strong wall that surrounded him.

"Are you for real, Brant Malone?" she whispered to the empty room.

Brant stared at the older man in blank astonishment. He thought of the beautiful young woman he had met earlier and what her father was proposing to do to her.

"You really are a no-good son of a—"

J.C. held up his hand. "That's no way to talk to your future father-in-law."

"You can forget that garbage," Brant said emphatically, coming to his feet. "Look, the meal and booze were great, the company okay up to a certain point... Now, I'd like a ride back to Dallas, if you don't mind."

"I do mind. Sit down."

The quiet voice was used to being obeyed, and Brant faced the fact that he wasn't in any position to be making demands. He was God knows where in north Texas, miles from any recognizable landmark, practically held prisoner by a man who was obviously insane. He sat down and waited.

J.C. studied him in silence for several minutes. He finally reached up and removed the cigar from his mouth before he said, "You find my daughter so unattractive?"

"That isn't the point. I have no intention of marrying anyone. Not ever. I'm not the marrying kind. I'm lousy husband material. Look, if you want to hire me as her bodyguard, I'll take the job. I can certainly understand your concerns. I'll move in here if it will make you feel any better. I'll sleep across her threshold every night. I won't let anyone harm a hair on her head." He waited, watching the other man warily.

"You will marry Denice," J.C. said in a firm, precise tone of voice.

Brant jumped to his feet. "Dammit! Haven't you heard a thing I said? Your daughter deserves to fall in love and marry the man of her dreams...not *me*. For God's sake, you don't want me marrying your daughter. You know nothing about me."

J.C. stared at him implacably. "I know everything about you, Malone...every single, solitary thing...

including the fact that Malone isn't even your real name.''

Brant slowly sat back down, his eyes never leaving the other man's face.

"I know you were born thirty-five years ago last May in Ann Arbor, Michigan, to Joseph and Rosalie Kowalski and that your birth certificate states your name as Michael Joseph Kowalski.

"I know your father couldn't keep a job, drank too much, and when he had nothing better to do, slapped you and your mother around for entertainment.

"I know that in February before you turned ten years old your father came home drunk one night in a rage and started beating your mother.

"I know you tried to stop him and he knocked you unconscious, and when you came to, your father was gone and your mother was dying. She died two days later and your father was arrested the same day. In the courtroom one week after your tenth birthday, you watched as they sentenced your father to life imprisonment. You managed to elude the juvenile authorities and left Ann Arbor that day on a freight train. You've never been back.

"I know everything you've done, every place you've been, who recruited you to work for them and why, and everything they taught you. I know why you changed your name and showed up back here in the States with fake credentials, a fake background and a fake résumé." He paused for a moment and took a draw on his cigar, then slowly blew the smoke out.

"Oh, and in case you're interested. Every one of the phone numbers you gave for references gave glowing reports about Brant Malone. Each one of them stated they were sorry to lose you." With careful deliberation he placed the cigar back in his mouth. "I'm sure they were."

He stared at the silent man seated across from him, puffed on the cigar a couple of times, then withdrew it, staring at the tip with concentrated interest.

"I know every woman you have ever been involved with, how long the relationship lasted, and why it broke up. I know what you had for breakfast on June 10 and whose bed you woke up in on August 18."

He paused for a sip of brandy, then raised his left brow and said, "And you will marry my daughter the day after Thanksgiving. These damn doctors may have miscalculated. I don't want to leave anything to chance."

Each word had bombarded Brant like a missile, burying itself deep inside of him. He had listened while his past had come hurtling back at him—the past he'd thought was safely buried and forgotten.

He felt numb and recognized the symptoms of shock. What sort of power did this man have that he could uncover what experts had gone to considerable time, effort and money to erase?

"I will not marry your daughter. I don't care what you've found out about me." He made his statement quietly in a voice devoid of expression.

The steady ticking of the mantel clock and an occasional log shifting in the fireplace were the only sounds in the room for several long minutes.

The older man sighed—a tired, worn-out sort of sigh. "Maybe you weren't listening, Malone. I said I know why you came back here and started all over. If you refuse to marry Denice I will see that you never work in the insurance field again. I can destroy your credibility so that no one will hire you, even after I'm gone.

"I can do that, and I believe you know it. I also believe you're a good enough judge of character to know I'll do it. I wouldn't want you to make the mistake of thinking I'm bluffing. That would be a massive miscalculation on your part, one that would prove to be irrevocable."

"Does Denice know anything about this?"

"Absolutely not. She never will. This is just between the two of us."

"How do you intend to get Denice to marry a complete stranger in less than two months?"

"You're going to court her."

Brant laughed, if the sound that came out of his throat could be designated as such. Bitterness almost consumed him. "Sorry, old man, but Prince Charming I'm not. I'm not into sweeping innocent young women off their feet. Perhaps you can force me to marry her, but I'm not going to pretend to be in love with her."

"All right. I'll handle that part of it."

Brant stood up. "May I go now?"

"Of course you may leave if you wish. Or we have plenty of guest rooms at your disposal."

"No thanks. For some strange reason, I don't think I would be able to fall asleep under your roof, Mr. Roberts."

"You'd better get used to the idea, or you're going to be spending a lot of sleepless nights after Thanksgiving."

The butler suddenly appeared at the door, and Brant realized J.C. had silently signaled him.

"Have Harris bring the car around. Mr. Malone wishes to return to the city tonight."

"Yes, sir."

J.C. walked Brant to the front door in silence.

Brant glanced at the man, then shook his head. "You know, it's a shame the doctors have given you such a short time. I would have liked the pleasure of making your life miserable."

J.C. began to laugh. "Why do you think I picked you, Brant? I had to find someone as tough as I am. I built this empire. It's going to take someone like me to hold it together."

"I can't think of a bigger insult than to be compared to you in any way." Brant's voice was low, but deadly.

J.C. clapped him on the back. "You'll do, son. You'll do."

He stood in the doorway and watched until the tail-lights of the limousine disappeared in the distance.

"The luckiest day in my life was the day Brant Malone walked in and applied for a job," J.C. muttered to himself, then walked back inside. Brant hadn't known about the ruthlessly thorough personnel checks J.C. insisted on for every employee. He'd learned his lesson years ago. Now he screened the people around him to make sure they could be trusted.

Much of Brant's early life was public record, and some of it, through educated guesswork, had been fairly easy to uncover. As far as his work for the U.S. government, it was always nice to have friends in high places—very high places.

J.C. stretched expansively, mighty pleased with himself. He had found a man who would be a fitting mate for his daughter and a worthy successor to him. The man was intelligent and cunning, and he was a lethal weapon to be turned on his enemies.

He wondered what Denice thought of him. It was too late to find out tonight. Over breakfast would be soon enough.

Was he pushing too much—insisting on a wedding in a couple of months?

He recalled his conversation last week with Harry Fairchild, his friend and personal physician for the past thirty years.

"J.C., if you don't get some weight off and cut down on those damn cigars and expensive booze, you're going to be dead before your next birthday!" Harry shook his head in disgust and motioned for J.C. to put on his shirt again.

"Can I have that in writing?" J.C. stood up, buttoned his shirt and stuffed it into his waistband.

Harry looked up from making notations in J.C.'s file. "What are you talking about?"

"Oh, nothing. Just a little project of mine that's been a little slow getting off the ground."

"What project?"

"Nothing professional, Harry." He wandered over to the window of the office and adjusted the shades, letting in sunlight. "I've been thinking about grandchildren. My grandchildren."

"Well, hell, J.C., I didn't even know Denice was getting married."

"Neither does she. She acts as though the thought has never entered her mind." He shook his head. "She's too wrapped up in those kids of hers at the hospital. They take up all her time and attention. She's trying to fulfill her maternal instinct with them. Doesn't even care that I'm left without any grandbabies.''

Harry laughed. ''My heart bleeds.''

''But I'm working on a plan.''

''Heaven have mercy. I'm not sure I want to hear it.''

''Don't worry, you aren't going to. But you don't think I'm long for this world, huh?''

''Did I say that? What I said was that you need to start taking better care of yourself, and you can start by losing some of that weight.'' He looked at his friend with a smile. ''Take it off, cut back on the cigars and alcohol, and you'll probably live to be a hundred.''

J.C. thought about that for a moment. He didn't need to live to be a hundred. Another twenty years would be enough if he got some grandkids fairly soon. ''All right, Harry. Draw me up a diet, send it to my chef and I'll stick to it. But if anyone should ask, it's a special diet because of my condition.''

''What condition?'' Harry asked suspiciously.

''My condition to encourage the production of grand-children in my old age, if you must know. No one else needs to know that.''

J.C. stood in the middle of the entryway and laughed at the memory of that visit. He was glad he had remembered to tell the chef to hold his diet for the night. Denice wasn't aware of the change in his eating habits, but of course she soon would be.

So what? He'd tell her he was trying to lose weight, which was the truth. If Malone thought it was because he was dying, so much the better.

Whistling under his breath, he went upstairs.

Three

Brant Malone arrived at work the next morning in a foul mood. He'd had a hell of a time going to sleep the night before, and for the first time in over a year his recurring nightmare had come back to haunt him. After he had finally fallen asleep again, he'd slept through his alarm.

It didn't improve matters when he arrived at his office to find it empty. Totally. Not a piece of furniture remained. Not even a scrap of paper.

He spun around and headed out the door and almost ran over his secretary, Joyce, whose clerical skills he shared with two other investigators. He waved his hand and tried to find something to say. She came to his rescue.

"Didn't anyone tell you, Mr. Malone? Your office has been moved upstairs."

"Since when? It was all here yesterday."

"Yes, sir, but the move was planned a few weeks ago. It must have been while you were out of town. I guess someone forgot to mention it to you."

"Yes—I guess *someone* did." He thought of J. C. Roberts, and could feel his blood pressure climb.

After five years of passing through the lobby of Roberts Fidelity & Guaranty Company he had grown accustomed to the life-sized portrait of Jefferson Calhoun Roberts. But when he'd stepped off the parking elevator that morning and crossed the lobby to the bank of high-rise elevators, he suddenly became aware of the face staring at him implacably from the lobby wall.

His future father-in-law.

His stomach rolled in protest, a reminder that Brant had not taken time to eat before he left home.

Brant had spent hours the night before trying to come up with a solution to his dilemma. He had a substantial amount of money invested. If he wanted to, he could forget the job and find some other line of work.

But why turn his life upside down because of J. C. Roberts?

And what would happen to Denice once her old man was gone? Of course the man had enemies. He was a master at cultivating them. A real expert. It was a damn miracle that no one had bumped him off before now.

He felt sorry for Denice. None of this was her fault. She was an innocent victim of a ruthless man's scheming manipulations.

He wondered what she was going to say about the marriage. What could she say? She would be given no more choice in the matter than he had been.

And what was she going to do when her father died? She loved him. She didn't have a clue that he was ill, and he wasn't giving her an opportunity to prepare herself for her loss.

Jefferson Calhoun Roberts was a first-prize, blue-ribboned unmitigated bastard.

To further make his day, the first person Brant saw when he stepped off the elevator onto the twentieth floor was Jefferson Calhoun Roberts in person.

Brant's secretary—or rather his former secretary—had explained that his office had been moved to the top floor. From now on he would have his own secretary.

"Good morning, Brant," J.C. said with an expansive smile. "You're looking well this morning." He stood with his hands clasped behind his back, rocking from his toes to his heels.

Aware of the number of people within earshot, Brant contented himself with muttering, "Good morning." He glanced around the luxurious offices of the top management of the firm, wondering why he would have offices up here and where his might be.

"Have you had breakfast this morning?"

Brant glanced around, and seeing no one close, growled, "You mean your spies haven't informed you as yet?"

"Hmm. I'd better warn Denice that you are definitely not a morning person." He started down the hallway. "You might as well join me in my office. I've ordered food to be sent in. I didn't take time to eat before I left home. Too much needs to be done, and there's not enough time to do it."

He motioned for Brant to follow.

Brant had never been on this floor before. There had never been a need. The majority of his work was in the field, which he enjoyed. He'd never seen himself as the type to sit behind a desk all day. He wondered what J.C. was up to now.

They passed by a door with a gold-plated nameplate that discreetly spelled out the name Brant Malone.

Brant stopped in his tracks.

J.C. also stopped, and walking over to the door, opened it. "We can go into my office through here, if you'd like. We have connecting doors. More convenient, you see, for a crash course in running a corporation."

Brant followed the older man through the door, dazed. The room they entered glowed from the early-morning sunlight coming through the eastern wall of glass. A massive desk and credenza were arranged against the north wall; a sofa and grouping of chairs and coffee table were against the south. There was still enough room to hold a square dance.

"I don't understand," Brant managed to say. "What is going on?"

"Nothing that we didn't discuss last night, Brant. Weren't you listening?"

"Last night! The only thing you announced last night was that I'm being forced to marry your daughter!"

"Forced is a little harsh, don't you think?"

"Do you prefer the word blackmailed?"

"I suppose forced will have to do." J.C. walked through the office and over to a door that blended perfectly into the paneled wall. It had been unnoticeable until he opened it. "Let's have breakfast. We can talk over coffee."

J.C.'s office was at the corner of the building, so that two walls were glass. Otherwise, the two offices were quite similar. A small table filled with covered dishes sat in front of the window, and J.C. motioned for Brant to sit down.

"We were talking about protecting Denice last night, Brant, both physically and financially. She's going to have to rely on the man in charge of this company to protect her investments. That man is you. You've learned a considerable amount about the company during the past five years. It shouldn't take you long to fill in the gaps of your education." He took a sip of black coffee. "And don't forget, I'm here to help you...as long as I can."

"Do you mean to tell me that you're making me head of the company?"

"Unofficially, yes. Officially, I will be in charge until the first of January when my retirement will be announced. You will be appointed my successor."

"But what about the stockholders?"

"Denice and I are the stockholders. I'm sure she'll see nothing strange about her husband taking over the company, particularly since you've been training for the position for some time."

Brant stared out the window, his thoughts whirling. "I don't believe this. Is this some kind of a joke?" He looked back at J.C. "You can't really be serious, can you? I suppose I can understand why you'd want me around to protect Denice, but this!" He waved his hand around the room. "I'm not a businessman. I don't know a damn thing about running a business. And I've never wanted to learn. It's too restrictive and confining."

J.C. grinned. "That's what you think. There is absolutely nothing like it, so don't knock it until you've tried it. You like to live on the edge—" He saw the slight change in Brant's expression. "Oh, I know that about you, too. You like to be tested, you like to take chances— well, here's the place to do it. You'll begin to understand power and the wielding of it, and you'll discover that you can't afford to make mistakes. There are too many people out there watching and waiting for one." He stopped talking and gave Brant a look of complete understanding.

"Try it. If you don't like it, I won't insist you do it. But give it a chance."

"You won't be around long enough to know if I like it or not. Then what?"

"Then you'll have to pick your own successor. You can do it. I did."

Brant began to eat; the food was too appetizing to pass up. Besides, he needed his strength. They ate in silence. When they were through, Brant poured them more coffee from the steaming carafe. With a slight frown, he asked, "How do you know I'm not marrying your daughter for your money?"

J.C. began to laugh, his stomach and jowls shook and his face reddened. He laughed until he was out of breath. Wiping his eyes, he looked at Brant and asked, "Are you?"

"Maybe."

"I don't care why you're marrying her, Malone, so long as you marry her."

"You don't give a damn about her feelings, do you?"

"Of course I do. I'm just not going to let her feelings change any of my plans. I hope she'll be very content with you."

"Did you tell her?"

"I didn't have a chance, but I intend to tonight. Why don't you plan to spend the weekend at our place. It will give both of you a chance to get better acquainted."

"Look, rather than force the issue, why don't you ask her how she feels about it? Give her a choice. Maybe there's someone else she'd rather marry."

"There isn't. I know. I don't think she's even given the matter any thought."

"Perhaps she doesn't want to get married."

"Well, it's up to you to change her mind."

"No. It's up to *you*. I refuse to marry a reluctant bride."

J.C. grinned. "I'll see what I can do." He stood up. "Ready for your first day on the new job?"

Brant got up more slowly. "As ready as I'll ever be." Secretly he wondered if the whole thing was a dream and that he would wake up soon in his hotel in Atlanta, the dream being the result of too much work, too little food, too much booze and an overactive subconscious. He shook his head. Not even a hyperactive imagination could have dreamed this one up.

He followed J. C. Roberts into the other room.

"Father, you seemed so quiet over dinner tonight. Is it because of your new diet?" Denice and J.C. sat in front of the study fireplace, sipping on coffee and enjoying the fire.

"Oh, the diet isn't bad. Harry said I'd probably enjoy it once I got used to it."

"I'm so proud of you for taking care of yourself. You're all I have, you know, and I do worry about you."

"I'm too mean to die, my dear. Not even the devil would have me."

Denice laughed, as he had meant her to. "What you are, Father, is a big old fake. Anyone who gets to know you well knows you're a real marshmallow inside."

J.C. looked down at his paunch and patted it lovingly. "Well, the marshmallow is beginning to show too much, I'm afraid."

They sat quietly in companionable silence for a while until Denice spoke again. "Something *is* bothering you, though. I can always tell when you're worrying about something. Is it anything you can talk about?"

J.C. had been staring intently into the fire, but her words made him shift his gaze to his daughter. She was a beautiful sight to behold. She wore a gold sweater dress that lovingly outlined her trim figure and brought out the gold in her hair and eyes. Her hair fell in soft waves around her face, the soft lighting in the room picking out strands of red and gold that were intermingled with the rich brown.

"What did you think of Brant Malone?"

The question surprised her. But perhaps that was her father's way of moving the subject away from whatever was troubling him.

"He seemed nice enough. Rather quiet."

"He's that, all right. But watch out when he has something to get off his chest!"

"What do you mean?"

"Oh, nothing." He finished the last of his coffee and set the cup back down. "He's taking over Roberts Fidelity & Guaranty the first of the year."

"Oh? And what will you do when you're not down there throwing your weight around?"

"Your sense of humor needs adjusting. I'm not amused."

"You will be once you get some of that weight off, you know."

"Do you really see me as a bully?"

Her eyes widened innocently. "You, a bully? Whoever would think of that word in connection with you?"

He eyed her suspiciously, then cleared his throat. "Maybe in my younger days. Now I'm nothing but a tame pussycat, content to sit in front of the fire on a chilly evening."

Denice laughed. "If that pathetic story is supposed to soften me up for something, it missed the mark."

J.C. straightened in his chair and leaned forward slightly, his face serious.

"I *am* getting too old for the daily pressures, I'm afraid. I'm tired of the fight. I want someone younger in there who won't give an inch."

"And Brant Malone is your choice."

"Yes."

"Then he must be quite a man. I've never known you to make a mistake in judgment."

"Only one. And I've had to live with it now for twenty years."

"What do you mean, Father?"

"Twenty years ago I was young and brash, and I thought I could conquer the world. I was doing a damn good job of it, too. But I was making some enemies. They didn't like my way of doing business and warned me off. I ignored them. So they killed your mother.''

"But, Father, Mother was killed in an automobile accident!'' Denice had gone white with his statement, and her denial was instinctive.

"It was no accident, Denice. I found a note in the mail the day we buried her, pointing out that I had been responsible for her death.'' He sounded tired and defeated as he talked about the past.

"I never even suspected,'' she said softly, almost to herself.

"No. There was no point. But I learned my lesson well, and I've never given anyone a chance to hurt someone I loved again. I never will, no matter what I have to do.''

She heard the pain in his voice and she hurt for him, but she could think of nothing to say to comfort him.

"For the past several weeks I've been receiving some threatening letters.''

Unconsciously Denice came to her feet. "Oh, no!''

"Yes. Someone is keeping close tabs on both of us. They told me everywhere we've gone and everything we've done, so that I know we're being watched.''

"How awful! And I had no idea.''

"That's why Harris takes you everywhere and stays with you except for your time in the hospital. There are people in the hospital who take over once you're inside.''

Denice stared at her father in amazement. "Just how many people do you have on your payroll, anyway?''

"Enough," her father muttered. He watched her as she slowly sat down and shakily poured herself another cup of coffee. "So I've come up with a new plan."

She glanced up at him and saw a grim smile of satisfaction that made her realize that his enemies had picked a relentless adversary.

"Brant Malone has the skills and the experience to deal with this sort of thing. I've explained the situation to him, and he agrees it calls for drastic measures. I believe they're worth it, though."

"What do you have in mind?"

"Brant has agreed to move out here with us, to be on the premises while I'm away. Not only will he be replacing me at the office, but here at home as well."

"But where will you be?"

"That's the beauty of my plan, you see. I'm going to leave the area, do some traveling, maybe take a cruise, just drop out of sight. It's me these people are really after, not you. They are threatening you to get me, don't you see? But if I'm not around, their threats won't do any good. And Brant will be here with you, so that I won't be leaving you unprotected."

Denice suddenly saw Brant's black eyes gazing at her with no expression, and shivered. Not a lonely executioner, but a lonely sentinel. Her instincts had been closer to the truth than she could have known.

"I've invited him out for the weekend, so that the two of you can get better acquainted. I suggested he move in during the Thanksgiving holidays."

"That's almost two months away, Father. Should you wait that long?"

"I don't want to make too many sudden changes, Denice. I wouldn't want to alert whoever it is to my plans. Right now Brant is learning the business. I want his move out here to seem like a natural progression of events."

Denice sat quietly for a few moments, her thoughts occupied with Brant. "He doesn't seem very friendly. What in the world will I say to him?"

"Let him take the lead. He understands what needs to be done."

"How long will he be here?"

"That depends on several things. I haven't been idle since these threats started coming. I have an ace investigation team working around the clock, tracing them, finding out who's behind them. We're going to get whoever it is, honey, don't worry. I just don't want to take any chances with your life while we're waiting."

She nodded, understanding so much about her father now. Denice walked over to her father's chair and leaned over, hugging him. "I love you, Father. So much."

"I'm glad, honey, real glad. Try to remember that in the coming months. Some of the arrangements may not be to your liking, but try to remember they're for your own good."

She laughed. "Just remember to take my medicine, no matter how bad it tastes. Is that the way to look at it?"

He thought of Brant and his anger at being forced into marriage. "Something like that."

Brant felt as though he'd been thrown into a bottom-less lake without any idea how to swim, and he was floundering. Papers lay in neat stacks all over the desk, and he tried to concentrate on the terms of the contract he was studying. This was not his scene.

He ran his hand through his hair, rearranging the already tousled waves.

"Hard at it, I see."

Brant looked up and saw J.C. standing in front of his desk. The man moved like a damn ghost, suddenly materializing and disappearing like a sprightly spirit.

"What time did you get here?"

Brant looked at his watch. It was almost ten o'clock. He sat back and stretched. "About six or so. I don't really remember."

"You're certainly taking your position seriously." J.C. pulled up a chair and sat down in front of the desk.

"That's what you're paying that enormous salary to me for." He rubbed his hand wearily across his eyes.

"You're earning it."

Hearing the dry tone, Brant looked up and grimaced. "I know." He tapped the papers he was reading. "You know I don't know a damn thing about these contracts and all their legal jargon. But from what I can figure out, whoever drew these papers up is trying to stick us with a surcharge in the fine print that is extortionary."

J.C. laughed. "Then tell them to blow it out their ear. And if you could find that little piece of information in all of those pages, you can rest assured no one is going to put anything over on you."

"You mean you knew it was in there?" J.C. nodded. "Then why the hell didn't you say something?"

"Because I wanted *you* to find it. And you did."

"And if I hadn't?"

J.C. shrugged. "Then we'd end up paying an exorbitant surcharge for the length of the contract."

Brant stared at the man in front of him. "You're insane," he finally muttered. "You're going to let me stumble around, make mistakes, cost the company money, and not do a damn thing about it."

"Everybody has to learn, Brant. I did. You did. We're both still learning. And we all make mistakes." He fished in his pocket and brought out a cigar. Lovingly lighting it, he puffed for a moment in quiet contemplation of the few pleasures left to him in life. They were enough, if he handled them right.

"Why don't you come out to the house for the weekend, look the place over, check the security and get better acquainted with Denice."

"Speaking of Denice, have you told her about your plans for us?"

"Yes, I did. Last night, as a matter of fact."

"I hope she told you to take a flying leap."

J.C. grinned around his cigar. "No, as a matter of fact, she didn't."

Brant stared at him in disbelief. "Are you telling me she has agreed to marry a man she doesn't even know?"

"Denice loves me. She knows I only want the best for her."

Brant leaned back in his chair, shaking his head. "I can't believe it." He gazed at the other man. "Did you tell her what the doctor said?"

"No. There's no reason to upset her at this point."

"Upset her! How the hell is she going to feel when you suddenly go. She won't have had any warning—no preparation."

"Sometimes that's the best way, you know. The grieving will be there. It can't be helped. Why prolong it by having her anticipate it?"

What could Brant say? It wasn't his business, but he was concerned for Denice. Maybe it was a good thing he was going to be with her. She would need somebody to lean on.

"When do you want me to come out?"

"Anytime. Friday night. Saturday morning. Whichever you prefer."

"I've got some things to finish up. I'll make it Saturday morning."

"Fine. Bring some casual clothes." J.C. stood up. "Do you enjoy horseback riding?"

"Yes."

"Denice loves to ride. She'll probably ask you to go with her. It will give you a chance to spend some time with her."

Brant found himself thinking ahead to the weekend. That was only two days away. Had all of this only happened in three days? His entire life had been turned upside down, shaken loose and let go, so that it was necessary to find the pieces and rebuild once more.

He had been forced to do that five years ago. He'd never expected to have to do it again.

Four

Denice heard the doorbell on her way down the stairs Saturday morning. "I'll get it, Morton," she called, hurrying to the door. It had to be Brant. They weren't expecting anyone else, and the guards at the gate would have called to report unscheduled guests.

She could feel the slight flush in her cheeks and hoped he wouldn't notice. She had noticed the bright sparkle in her eyes that morning while she put on her light makeup and had recognized that she was actually excited about their weekend guest. Not wanting to appear over-dressed, she had opted to wear an old pair of jeans and a cream sweater. She'd also put on her boots because she intended to go riding when the weather warmed up a little later in the day.

Reaching the door, she opened it and smiled at the man who stood there. He wore black form-fitting jeans that left no doubt about his masculinity and a black cable-knit sweater that emphasized the wide expanse of his heavily muscled chest and arms.

"Don't tell me, let me guess," she said. "You must be Zorro." She stepped back. "Please come in. I'm so glad you left your mask at home. It's so much less formal."

Brant had expected to be met at the door by the butler; he wasn't prepared to be greeted by a vivacious, sparkling Denice, wearing a sweater whose color was the soft cream of her warm complexion and a pair of jeans that made him want to run his hands over the pockets to make sure they weren't just painted on.

Her greeting further disconcerted him, and he stepped into the hallway without saying a word.

She looked past him and saw a Corvette sitting out front. She wasn't in the least surprised to see that it was black. "If you've left your keys with your trusty steed, I'll have Harris put it in the garage."

He glanced over his shoulder. "Yes, the keys are in the car."

Fantastic. He is capable of the simple declarative sentence, she thought. *In time, perhaps he can be encouraged to greater feats of linguistic skills—say the compound-complex sentence. Who knows? Someday maybe whole paragraphs!*

"Have you had breakfast?" she asked with a mischievous grin.

Why did she look at him with so much amusement? Had he forgotten to shave? Unconsciously he ran his hand through his hair and remembered he had forgotten to get a haircut. He wasn't sure what to say to her. What could he say to a strange woman whom he was expected to marry in a few weeks?

"Yes, I have. But I wouldn't mind having some more coffee."

She tucked her arm in his and began to walk him toward the dining room. "If you don't mind, I'll have breakfast while you drink your coffee. I slept in this morning."

Her breast nudged against his arm, and the scent of her perfume wafted around him. Brant could feel his body stiffening in reaction to her nearness. She was certainly letting him know she was going to be a willing bride! Maybe she was relieved that her father had gone out and bought her a husband. Saved her the trouble.

Breakfast was set out in a buffet style, and Brant found himself joining Denice in another breakfast. He'd only had toast and coffee. The food prepared could have fed a dozen people.

When they were seated, Brant asked, "Where's J.C.?"

She looked up in surprise. "Oh, didn't he tell you? He flew to Pittsburgh this weekend to watch the Cowboys play the Steelers."

"Oh."

The conversation lapsed once more.

Brant wished he could think of something to say to her. She seemed friendly enough, but he found the situation awkward, to say the least.

Denice wished she could think of something to say to him. He seemed to be trying to be friendly, but wasn't sure how. She felt as though she was trying to befriend a Doberman trained to guard her. As a matter of fact, she thought a Doberman would probably be easier to get to know.

"Do you ride?" she finally asked, beginning to feel a little desperate for conversation.

"Yes."

"Would you like to see something of the place after breakfast? Horseback is about the best way to really explore the area."

"Sounds all right to me."

She sighed with relief. Well, that would take care of a few hours. Maybe by the time they'd spent a little more time together, he'd begin to relax.

After they had finished eating, Denice said, "Harris has probably taken your luggage to your room. Why don't I show you where you'll be staying." She glanced down at his black Italian-made shoes. "Did you bring any boots?"

"Yes."

"Don't tell me, let me guess. They're black."

"Yes."

"What is this obsession you have with wearing black?"

"It saves trying to coordinate a wardrobe."

"I suppose that's true, but doesn't it get a little boring after a while?"

"Not to me."

She shrugged. Maybe he felt it fit the part. Most watchdogs were black, now that she thought about it.

Once out on horseback, Denice no longer worried about her guest. Nothing ever bothered her as long as she could ride. She took him around to some of her favorite places and pointed out the boundary lines of the property. As they rode, they came across several of the cattle her father owned.

"I wasn't aware your father did any ranching."

"He does all kinds of things. He's into real estate, insurance, television, radio, satellite communication, ranching, farming—"

"And do you keep up with all of it?"

"No. It keeps him occupied, and that's what's important."

"But you don't mind spending the money, I'm sure."

She glanced around at him, surprised at the remark and the ironic tone. They were following a trail through a grove of trees, but it was wide enough for them to ride abreast of each other.

"I don't really think about his money all that much, Brant. It's just there. It's always been there. I use it if I need it. It's certainly nice to have, but otherwise, I don't pay that much attention to it."

"Many women would use it to jet all over the world, visit all the popular resorts, buy the latest fashions, attend all the openings."

"I'm not most women. I'm very content with my life."

"Do you like working with children?"

Her eyes lit up. "Yes, I adore them. The hardest part for me to adjust to was the pain they endure. I want to take it away from them. Some of the things I have them do actually creates more pain for them, but it's necessary to help them recover."

She glanced over at him, enjoying the way he sat on the horse. She didn't know where he'd learned to ride, but he rode as though he'd been born in a saddle.

"Have you ever lived on a ranch?" she asked with sudden intuition.

He glanced at her in surprise. "Yeah, as a matter of fact, I have. What made you ask that question?"

"Oh, something about the way you ride. Where were you?"

"Wyoming. It was many years ago. I was just a kid looking for a job and a place to live. I found an old rancher who needed some help but didn't have much money. I stayed with him, went to school and did all I could to help him survive."

"No wonder you don't like winter. Wyoming can get pretty bitter, can't it? Even worse than upstate New York."

"Yes."

"How long did you stay there?"

"About six years. Until Jake was killed. He was thrown from his horse and broke his neck."

"How awful!"

"Yeah, it was. But it happened a long time ago."

They rode in silence for a while until Denice finally asked, "What did you do after that?"

"Went into the service."

"Did you go overseas?"

He turned his head and looked at her. "What is this, twenty questions?"

She felt the heat rise in her cheeks, and she recognized how rude she'd been with all of her questions. "I'm sorry. I didn't mean to pry."

They rode in silence for almost a mile before Brant spoke. "How do you feel about my coming out here?"

"You mean this weekend or the fact that you'll be moving in at Thanksgiving."

Moving in. That's a polite way of putting it. "I mean," he said with slow deliberation, "how do you feel about marrying me?"

Denice unconsciously jerked the reins, and her horse reared slightly and snorted. "Marrying you! What in the world are you talking about?"

Brant registered her shocked surprise and realized that once again J. C. Roberts had managed to set him up. He hadn't told her about the marriage. Instead, he had invited Brant to visit, then disappeared for the weekend. He was a totally unprincipled bastard.

He was also Denice's father, he reminded himself.

Brant looked around and said, "Why don't we rest for a while. It looks to me as though we need to get some things straight."

He swung out of the saddle with accustomed ease, then walked around to where she still sat staring at him in stunned disbelief. He reached up and, placing his hands on her waist, lifted her out of the saddle. She felt light, and he brought her against him, allowing her to slide slowly down his body until her boots touched the ground.

Her perfume filled his senses, and he inhaled, enjoying the smell of her. He liked the feel of her, too, and he wondered about the taste of her.

His hands slid from her waist to the back pockets of her jeans, where they slipped inside, cupping her firm derriere in the palms of his hands. He pulled her intimately against him.

Slowly lowering his head, he found her mouth with his. She tasted of mint and roses, and his hands moved up to hold her firmly against him while he drank his fill of her. His hands explored the soft contour of her back, finding the slight indentation of her spine, the swell of her hips.

Meanwhile his mouth moved over hers in a sensuous exploration all its own. He nudged her mouth open with his tongue, and when he gained entrance he claimed complete possession.

Denice had never been kissed in such an intimate manner before, had never been claimed quite so insistently and had never reacted to any man the way she was reacting to Brant Malone, who had just announced he was going to marry her!

She forced her hands between them, pushing against his chest. The muscles felt like polished marble. They didn't give. His arms felt like steel bands around her, and she discovered she couldn't move. Not unless he wanted her to move.

He felt her hands on his chest, their warmth searing through him as though permanently branding their imprint.

Brant forced himself to loosen his hold on her as he became aware of her resistance. He discovered that for a few moments he had lost control of himself. He had wanted her with a tearing, gut-wrenching pain of desire that threatened to destroy his self-control.

He stepped back slightly. He felt her trembling and he braced her with his arms. "I'm sorry. I didn't mean to scare you."

She looked up into his black eyes, startled at the burning light in their depths. Hesitantly she reached up and placed her palm on his lean cheek, feeling a muscle jerk along his jaw. "You didn't scare me," she managed to say.

"You're trembling."

"Am I?" She glanced around, a little dazed. "I'm not used to this," she tried to explain.

"To what? Being kissed?"

She tried to laugh, and it came out a little shaky. "Was that what that was? I wasn't sure."

"Would it do any good to say I didn't intend that to happen?"

She nodded. "I can understand that. It wasn't what I had in mind when I suggested we go for a ride, either." She suddenly remembered what he had said. "Why did you mention marriage earlier?"

He took her hand and led her over to a dead tree that looked as though it had been resting there for some time. He sat down and urged her to sit down beside him.

"Exactly what did your father tell you about the reasons for me coming out here?"

Her sherry-colored eyes stared at him in bewilderment. "But don't you know?"

"No. I have no idea what he told you."

"He explained about the threatening notes he'd been receiving. Someone has been watching us. They keep telling him everything we've done and every place we've been. He said you were going to move out here until they found out who was doing it."

Brant stared off in the distance. The old man could still surprise him. He wondered if there really were threats being made. If so, J.C. was really playing his cards close to his chest, not even telling *him*.

"Then he didn't tell you that I'm going to marry you."

Her heart did a triple somersault in her chest and began to keep a march time. Her reaction wasn't due so much to what he had said, but the way he had said it with an implacable certainty that would not be easily discouraged.

"But why marry me? Why can't you just guard me?"

He thought about that question for several minutes. He didn't have the answer. Only J.C. knew why marriage was mandatory.

"I don't know, but I have a few ideas."

"Such as?"

"For some reason he must feel that there's a leak in the security around this place, or he wouldn't want someone with you at the house. If the security has been breached, then you're most vulnerable when you're alone at night. That's where I'll come in."

The thought of spending her nights with Brant Malone caused a tingling within her as though she'd received a low-voltage shock to the system. "And you agreed to this?"

He stared at her for a moment, unsure of what to say. She looked so vulnerable, so bewildered, and he didn't want to hurt her. But he wasn't going to lie to her, either. "I wasn't given much choice."

"Oh," she said without expression. That explained so much. Once again her father had made a pronouncement and everyone was expected to obey. "But if the matter was left to you, you wouldn't get married."

"No."

"I see." How could she possibly feel rejected? She hadn't been consulted, and had no intention of marrying him, but for some reason knowing he didn't want to marry her was painful. She felt as though she had asked and been turned down, but that wasn't the case at all. The fact was that he intended to marry her, despite his feelings about the matter.

How insulting. She had never had a particularly inflated sense of her own importance, but Denice recognized that she had a considerable amount of love to give to the right man.

"How much is my father bribing you to marry me?"

Her carefully amused tone didn't quite mask her hurt and resentment. "I think my promotion was in the nature of a bribe."

"Something you've worked for these past five years, I take it?"

"No. As a matter of fact, I prefer what I was doing to what I'm expected to do now."

"Then why did you agree to marry me?"

"Let's just say he made me an offer I couldn't refuse."

"And if I don't want to marry you?"

"I really don't believe that will change anything."

Denice jumped up and strode over to her horse. She mounted while Brant followed more slowly and climbed on his horse. She looked at Brant and wished she hadn't met him in this way. Perhaps if they had met through mutual friends they might have had a chance. But not like this. Never like this.

"Well, Mr. Malone, whatever the offer was, I'll double it. I don't want to marry you and have no intention of doing so." She dug her heels lightly into the side of her mount and galloped back to the house.

"All right, J.C., I did what I could to sell her on your damned idea, but she isn't buying. You'll have to deal with her in your own way."

Brant followed the trail more slowly, content to have some time to himself. He could still remember how she had felt in his arms, her breasts pressed tightly against his chest, still taste the warmth of her lips under his, still hear the soft sigh she gave when he pulled her into his arms. His palms felt etched with the shape of her shapely bottom, and he groaned.

Denice Roberts was one hell of a woman.

Five

Brant was at work on Monday morning when two small oblong pieces of cardboard fell on the desk in front of him. He looked up to find J.C. standing opposite him.

Brant leaned back in his chair and studied the man in front of him. "I was impressed with how well you explained everything to Denice," Brant said in a casual tone of voice. "It made my weekend so much more comfortable."

"Morton said you left right after lunch on Saturday."

"That's right, I did. Denice sent down word that she'd developed a headache while we were out and wouldn't be down to eat. After a delightful meal enjoyed in isolated splendor, I decided I'd had all the fun I could handle for one weekend, so I came back to town." He pointed to the two objects J.C. had dropped on the desk. "Care to explain what these are?"

"What do they look like?"

Brant straightened in his chair and picked up two tickets to a musical production. He frowned.

J.C. spoke. "Denice is expecting you to pick her up at six o'clock. You have dinner reservations at six-thirty. The play begins at eight-fifteen."

Brant studied the older man for a moment, an impassive look on his face. "Denice is expecting me to take her to dinner and to a play—" he glanced down at the tickets he held in his hand "—tonight?"

"Yes."

"You know, J.C., I seem to have developed a deplorable lack of trust in your words." Brant leaned back in his chair once more and stared at the man across from him. "Somehow I find your news difficult to believe."

"She just needs some time to get used to the idea. While she's getting used to it, you might as well get into the habit of escorting her places—such as to the theater and the symphony—that sort of thing."

"The symphony! Me? Look, J.C., I've never been to a symphony or a play in my life."

"Congratulations." J.C. turned and walked back toward his office. "Six o'clock," he said without looking around.

Brant's glare was wasted on the man leaving his office. Damn. He knew he'd be there at six o'clock to face Denice. What he couldn't understand was his own behavior. Was he afraid he would hurt her feelings if he didn't show up? Why was he so damned concerned about Denice Roberts's feelings? It wasn't his fault J. C. Roberts was her father. He shook his head, disgusted with himself.

Picking up a letter in the stack of mail in front of him, he began to read through it.

The last thing Denice wanted to do was attend a musical comedy with Brant Malone. He probably didn't know how to laugh.

If she were honest, she was also embarrassed to see him again after their last disastrous meeting. How did one behave around the man your father insisted you were going to marry?

"I don't even want to get married," she announced to her bedroom.

Marriage was so intimate. She'd never thought of herself in connection with a personal relationship, shying away from the idea of getting close to a man, either physically or emotionally.

But would she ever become close to Brant Malone? He was so aloof. She couldn't imagine sitting down and discussing some domestic problem with him.

Her father said he had a good head for business—very quick-witted and shrewd. Those would be important qualities to J.C., but did they make admirable traits in a mate?

Somehow she doubted it.

Denice glanced at her watch. It was almost six. Time to go downstairs.

The doorbell rang just as she reached the top of the steps, and she watched as Morton opened the door for Brant.

The light from the chandelier glinted on his black hair, and Denice smiled. He'd gotten his hair cut, the unruly wave properly combed away from his forehead, giving him an impeccable, well-groomed appearance. He had also dressed in a suit for the occasion—a well-tailored, immensely flattering suit. Black, of course.

She started down the stairs, and he glanced up. Their eyes met, and she paused for a moment, temporarily disoriented. What was it about his eyes that created such a reaction within her? For a flash of a moment she had detected a gleam of—what? Warmth? Interest? She couldn't be certain. It wasn't indifference.

Denice walked over to him and held out her hand. With an impish grin, she said, "You're a very brave man, Mr. Malone."

Brant's appraisal of her appearance in her turquoise gown caused her heart to leap uncertainly. He took her hand, his larger one enveloping hers in a warm grip. He lifted one brow slightly in inquiry.

"You keep coming back for more abuse from the Roberts family," she explained lightly.

A slow smile appeared on his tanned face, his gaze meeting hers in wry understanding. "So it would seem," he admitted. "Are you ready?"

"Yes. Will I need a jacket?"

He shrugged. "It's up to you. You know what Texas weather is like."

"I think October is my favorite time of the year. I'll be daring and hope the warm weather holds."

Brant placed his hand in the small of her back and walked her out to his car, then helped her inside without comment.

They had driven several miles before Denice accepted the fact that Brant wasn't going to say anything more. Unless she was resigned to spending the entire evening with him in silence, she would have to be the one to initiate a conversation.

"I want to apologize for my behavior Saturday," she said abruptly, ending the silence. Her need for honesty between them had overcome her embarrassment.

He glanced at her from the corner of his eye. "For what?"

"For being so rude to you. I'm sorry I left you on your own."

"I managed to survive."

"I just want you to know that I don't usually behave that way."

"I didn't think you did. A woman doesn't often find out she's marrying a man she doesn't know."

"I hope it doesn't offend you when I say that I have no intention of marrying you."

"I'm not offended."

"But rather than make a scene this morning when Father informed me you were taking me out tonight, I decided to wait and discuss the matter with you."

"Discuss what matter?" he asked, having a little trouble following her.

"Our not getting married."

"Oh."

"I've been giving the matter considerable thought. You know, all you have to do is to convince Father you won't marry me and that will be the end of it."

"I hope this doesn't offend you," he gently mocked her, "but I've already tried that. It didn't work."

She was quiet for a few minutes. "I just wish I could understand why he's so insistent."

"So do I."

"It's silly to think I need a guard in my room. If necessary, I could always get a Doberman."

"A much less complicated plan, I'll admit."

"Then you agree?"

"Absolutely."

Denice relaxed against the comfortable seat and sighed softly. "I feel so much better about everything now that we understand each other."

"I don't think that was ever the problem. J.C. is the one who needs convincing."

"I'm not worried," Denice said confidently. "Father has never insisted I do anything I was firmly against."

"You have no idea how relieved I am to hear that." He drove for a while in silence. "So what do you want to do now?"

"About what?"

"Tonight. Do you still want to have dinner and go to the theater?"

"Only if you do."

He drove for a few moments in silence. "We need to eat sometime," he pointed out slowly, "and since we already have the tickets—"

"I can't see you enjoying musical comedy, Brant."

"We can always find out, can't we?"

The conversation cleared the air, and by the time Brant and Denice reached the restaurant and ordered, they were chatting like old friends. Denice managed to draw Brant into discussing his new position and how he felt about it.

Eventually he began to discuss some of his more difficult cases with her.

Denice found herself watching him across the table, the soft candlelight emphasizing the strong bone structure of his face. How could she ever have thought his eyes had no expression? They sparkled and glowed, and she felt warmed by the flame she saw within them.

As she listened she realized that this man would never accept anything he hadn't earned. Whatever his reasons for agreeing to a marriage, he wasn't after money or position. She wasn't sure how she knew that, but it was true nonetheless.

She laughed at his droll wit, wondering why she'd ever thought he had no sense of humor.

Brant loved her laugh, and he found himself waiting to hear it. It was soft and tinkling, like tiny bells on a wind chime, innocent and endearing.

They were almost late for the theater.

Perhaps it was the mood they had brought from the restaurant, but Brant and Denice found the play very entertaining, chuckling over the humor and, by occasional shared glances, recognizing their enjoyment was enhanced because of the other one's presence.

Denice was sorry to see the play end. She admitted to herself that she was reluctant to have the evening end as well. She had enjoyed this glimpse of Brant that she was certain few people had ever seen.

"Are you ready to go home?" he asked once they were in the car. The streetlamps cast a shadow, effectively masking his expression. His voice was carefully neutral.

"Not really," she admitted. "Are you?"

He shifted in the seat so that he was turned toward her. Leaning forward slightly, he placed the back of his fist against her cheek and lightly rubbed its satiny softness with his knuckles. "No. What would you like to do now?"

Denice found it hard to concentrate on what he was saying when he touched her. "I know of a quiet lounge where they play soft music." She looked at him uncertainly. "Do you like to dance?"

"I'm discovering all kind of things I enjoy doing—with you." He turned his hand and cupped her cheek and jawline.

Denice watched, mesmerized as he leaned closer to her. She could have pulled away with no effort; his hand barely rested on the side of her face. The light suddenly fell on his face, and she saw his eyes, capturing her in their mysterious glow.

His mouth touched hers lightly, delicately, with no pressure to mar the gentle mood of the moment. She could smell his after-shave, and it reminded her of pine-scented forests and ocean breezes, of the wildness of nature and freedom. A feeling of excitement began to grow from deep within her as though his touch set off tiny electrical charges in her most secret places.

Denice didn't recognize the symptoms because no one had ever made her feel that way before. Brant's kiss two days before had been an initiation into another world—the world of sensual pleasure.

Her hands came up from where they lay in her lap. She wanted to touch him, feel him closer to her. Brant gradually increased the pressure, and her mouth opened to his as her arms came up around his neck.

She felt so good in his arms. So right. Everything else was forgotten—her father and his plans, the differences between the two of them and the fact that neither wanted to make a commitment.

Brant forced himself to straighten, his lips slowly and reluctantly leaving hers. He looked down at her and watched as her long, thick lashes slowly raised, her rare golden eyes focusing on him with difficulty.

"Where is this place you're talking about?" he asked in a husky voice.

Denice brought her hands from around him, surprised that she had been holding him so close. "Oh, uh, we'll need to get on the expressway and go toward downtown." She sat back, a little breathless.

He started the car, shifted, then reached out and placed his hand over hers. "I've enjoyed being with you tonight."

"I've enjoyed it, too," she said quietly.

"Do you go out much?"

"Not really."

"Your father said you don't date anyone in particular. I don't understand why."

"Oh, I suppose it's because I don't have that much time. After a day at the hospital, I'm ready to go home and relax."

"But don't you want to marry someday and have a family?"

She didn't know how to answer that. Until last Saturday, she had never spent much time thinking about it. Since then, that's all she had thought about.

"Oh, I don't know. How about you? Do you want a wife and family?"

"No," he said without hesitation.

"You sound very adamant."

"Some men aren't cut out for the domestic scene. I'm one of them."

"And yet you seemed to be resigned to marrying me."

"I had no choice."

"You keep saying that, but I firmly believe we all have choices in life."

"All right. Then let me say I didn't care for my other choices."

Her infectious laugh filled the car. "How flattering. I'm the lesser of several evils."

He grinned. "Something like that."

She turned her hand so that she could grasp his. "I'm glad it didn't come down to that. I believe I much prefer you as a friend than a husband."

"Thank you. I think."

"It was definitely a compliment. It was only as I said it that I realized I do feel that I have made a friend tonight. You seem to understand how I feel."

He nodded. "I do. And I care about what happens to you. I want you to know that. If you ever need someone, please feel that you can call me."

She brought their enfolded hands to her face and brushed his hand against her cheek. "Thank you."

They located the small lounge Denice had mentioned and went inside. Small tables dotted the dimly lit room, forming a half circle around a fair-sized dance floor. A three-piece combo provided music that was low, slow and enticing. Several couples were on the dance floor, taking advantage of the opportunity to hold each other close.

No sooner had Brant given the waitress their order than he stood up and held his hand out to Denice. She took it, and he led her onto the floor. Pulling her into his arms, he slowly swayed to the music.

Denice didn't enjoy being held close while dancing. At least she had never cared for it until now. Brant's lead was strong and easy to follow, and she relaxed and allowed him to lead her.

She lifted her head from his shoulder and looked up at him. "You dance very well."

"You wouldn't say that if you had suggested a place that played country or rock music. My skills are severely limited."

She grinned, her dimple suddenly appearing. "Something tells me that you haven't been a hermit all these years. Don't you have a special person in your life?"

Because she was pressed so tightly against him, she felt him tense, and suddenly she wished she knew when to keep her mouth shut. She had only been trying to make conversation so that she wouldn't be so aware of his taut length against her.

"No."

"But at least you haven't sat at home all alone, night after night," she insisted, her voice carefully light and cheerful. She could feel him relax slightly.

"Most of my social activities have had some relation to my work. I've received some of my best leads over drinks, dinner or a dance."

She smiled up at him, deliberately seductive. "I just bet you have, Mr. Malone. I can't imagine a woman not wanting to tell you anything you wanted to know."

He threw back his head and laughed, a full, rich sound that grabbed at her heart and squeezed it. "Oh, Denice, you're something else." He shook his head.

The music ended and the band took a break. Brant and Denice walked back to the table and sat down.

Some perverse need to better understand him prompted Denice to ask, "Haven't you ever been in love, Brant?"

He'd been staring down into his drink, and he raised his head suddenly at her question.

"Why do you want to know?"

"Because you fascinate me. You're so brooding and mysterious. A man with a past." She smiled. "And you hate questions."

"That doesn't seem to bother you much."

"Only when I don't get the answers."

"You're more like your father than I realized."

"Somehow I don't think you meant that as a compliment."

He thought about that for a moment. "Oh, your dad isn't so bad. I can't say I agree with his methods, but he's certainly accomplished a great deal in one lifetime. I'm always coming across something that he's originated that continually amazes me. He's got a mind like a steel trap. Spots other people's vulnerabilities and uses them."

"Is that what he did with you?"

"Do you think I'm vulnerable?"

"Not to look at you, no. But I have a feeling that you'd be vulnerable in love. If you ever gave your love to someone, you'd be there for them, no matter what."

He finished his drink and signaled for another one. "Then you'd be wrong. I've never been able to help anyone I've ever loved. So I learned not to love anyone. It's safer all the way around." He stood up. "Care to dance?"

She followed him out on the dance floor, and they circled in silence for a while.

"What? No more questions?" he finally said in a low voice in her ear.

Denice was no longer thinking about Brant and his mysterious past. The present was too inviting. She could have spent hours in his arms, feeling the controlled strength of his body as he neatly sidestepped others on the dance floor. She enjoyed the way he held her, his hand in the center of her back, guiding her as he moved and turned.

It would be very easy to lose sight of the fact that this man was not what she wanted in life.

She shook her head. "No more questions. I'm just going to forget everything but the here and the now."

"A philosophy I strongly recommend."

Denice relaxed and flowed with the music, content to be in Brant's arms.

Six

Brant and Denice eventually left the small club and started the long drive to her home in contented silence. She had enjoyed the evening. It seemed like something out of a dream—the laughter, the conversation, the closeness they had shared. Denice rested her head on the back of the seat and closed her eyes, already storing memories of their time together.

"Denice, we're home."

Brant's low voice wafted through her thoughts, and she opened her eyes slowly and looked around. They sat in front of her home. She must have fallen asleep. She didn't even remember pausing at the gate.

"Would you like to come in?" she asked politely, spoiling it slightly with a small yawn.

"No. You need to get some sleep."

"So do you. Look at the drive you still have ahead of you."

He walked around the car and helped her out.

"Would you like to stay here tonight?"

His eyes widened in pretended shock. "Why, Miss Roberts. I can't believe what I'm hearing," he said in a slow drawl. "The woman who refuses to marry me is inviting me to spend the night with her?"

She could feel the heat of a blush in her cheeks. "You know very well what I mean. We have plenty of room."

Brant paused in front of the door and looked around at the massive home. "I dare say you do. I understand the Hilton Inn calls here when they're overbooked."

She grinned. "I used to think you had no sense of humor," she confided.

His face sobered. "There are times when I don't."

"Well, I'm glad you shared it with me tonight. I had a marvelous time."

He took her hand. "So did I."

"Are you sure you won't come in for some coffee or a drink?"

"Positive. I see enough of J.C. at the office. I don't need to be grilled on our evening activities tonight."

"Are you going to tell him of our decision tonight?"

"I thought I would allow you that honor and privilege."

"Do I detect a note of cynicism in your voice?" she teased.

"Let's just say that I don't have as much faith in your persuasive powers as you do."

She patted his hand. "You can count on it. I don't know what he's up to, but he's going to find out we aren't going to stand for it."

"Whatever you say."

Denice went up on tiptoe and kissed him lightly on the mouth. "Go home and get some rest. And thank you again. I will never forget this evening."

Brant returned to his car and drove away. He doubted that he would ever forget the evening, either. He had never known anyone remotely like Denice Roberts. He knew he'd never forget her.

Denice went through her bedtime preparations absently and crawled into bed. She went to sleep thinking about Brant Malone.

"How did your evening go?"

Brant looked up from his morning mail with a slight frown. "J.C., would it be asking too much for you to at least tap on the door or clear your throat or something. Your ability to suddenly appear in front of me and speak has startled me out of a few rather treasured years."

"Just goes to show you how out of shape you are. That sort of absorption would have gotten you killed a few years ago."

Brant leaned back in his chair with a patient expression on his face. "Has it ever occurred to you that that was one of the reasons I changed occupations? I don't want to live that way anymore."

"You haven't answered my question."

"I enjoyed the evening. Now then, is it all right if I get back to work? I have five days' accumulated mail here that needs to be answered today."

"Relax, my boy. No need to solve all the world's ills before noon. You need to learn to enjoy yourself more."

"And you're just the man who's going to teach me, I take it."

"I'll do my best."

"I can hardly wait."

"Denice seemed to be in good spirits this morning. I told you it wouldn't take her long to get used to the idea."

"I hate to burst your balloon, J.C., but Denice hasn't gotten used to a thing. We discussed it last night and are agreed that we don't intend to get married."

J.C. sat down and pulled out a cigar. "You don't, huh?" He carefully lit his cigar and leaned back, puffing contentedly. The news didn't seem to bother him, which tended to bother Brant. But he refused to let it show.

"No, we don't."

"How do you intend to avoid it?"

"It's a little difficult to have a wedding without a bride or groom."

"That's a point."

Brant picked up one of the documents on his desk. "Was there something else you wished to discuss? If not, I have work to do."

"You seem to be getting into the flow of the business."

"I try, J.C. Anytime you'd like to send me back out into the field, please don't hesitate."

J.C. chuckled. After puffing for a moment in silence, he said, "When do you intend to see Denice again?"

Brant glanced up in surprise. "I don't, why?"

"You mean last night was it for the two of you?"

"I don't see any point in furthering our acquaintance under the circumstances. You'd be better off spending your time looking for someone Denice wants to marry rather than sitting here visiting with me."

"You mean you don't care what happens to her after I'm gone?"

Brant slammed the papers on his desk. "Of course I care, dammit! But there's not a hell of a lot I can do about it, now, is there? If she doesn't want to marry me, I'm sure as hell not going to force the issue."

"But if you spend more time with her, let her get to know you better, maybe she won't be so against marrying you."

"Why should I do that? I have no desire to obtain a wife."

"We aren't talking about a wife in the abstract. We're talking about your marrying Denice."

"I'm aware of that."

"You still insist you don't want to marry her?"

"I don't want to marry anyone."

J.C. got up from his chair and wandered over to the connecting door to his office. "You might want to consider what it would take to make you change your mind."

Brant stared at the closing door in frustration. Why wouldn't the man leave it alone? Brant had no desire to get married. He didn't need anyone and he didn't want to need anyone. He certainly wasn't the kind of man Denice deserved.

He forced himself to concentrate on the work at hand.

Denice was almost asleep when the phone by her bed rang. She rolled over and and sleepily answered.

"H'lo?"

"I'm sorry. I didn't realize it was so late. I'll talk to you some other time."

She sat up in bed and clutched the phone tighter. "No, don't hang up. This is Brant, isn't it?"

"Yes."

"How are you?"

"Tired. I worked through the evening without stopping to eat. I should have realized you'd be asleep by now."

"Oh, I wasn't asleep. I mean, not really." She wasn't sure what to say or why he had called. "What's keeping you working such long hours?"

"Trying to learn the business. Trying to stay one step ahead of the game. Right now I'm lucky to stay even."

"I'm sure Father didn't intend you to keep these hours."

"Who knows what your father intends or doesn't intend?" he said in a disgusted tone.

"Did you talk with him today?"

"I talk to him every day. I also have to listen to him every day."

She laughed. "He can be a real pain at times, I know."

"Well, look, I'll let you go. I happened to be thinking of you and thought I'd see how you were."

"I'm fine." She thought for a moment. "Would you like to come out for dinner tomorrow night?"

There was a long pause, and she waited, almost holding her breath.

"I never pass up a free meal. Especially at the Roberts residence. The chef is unbeatable."

"It's nice to know there's an irresistible pull for you here," she said, a smile in her voice.

He chuckled. It was the warm sound that she had discovered to be so attractive the night before. "What time?"

"How about six?"

"Fine. See you then."

She waited until she heard him hang up and then reluctantly replaced the phone. She lay there for a long time before finally falling asleep.

For the next several weeks, Brant spent more and more time with Denice. He discovered that he didn't mind the symphony at all. She also went with him to a couple of basketball games. One weekend they drove to Galveston and walked along the beach. They stayed at a hotel overlooking the water, their rooms at opposite ends of the hall.

Brant had never spent so much uninterrupted time with a woman before. He found her fascinating. She seemed to get so much enjoyment out of little things: watching the gulls fly around the beach, looking for shells washed up by the tide, building a sand castle.

He found it hard to relate the woman he was beginning to know with J. C. Roberts.

Brant did notice that J.C. was definitely thinning down, and he wondered if it was due to his health. He could think of no other reason. Whenever Brant was around him, J.C. continued to eat the rich food his chef prepared so well.

There was no need to bring up the subject, but Brant couldn't help but wonder what Denice would do when

J.C. succumbed to his mysterious ailment. He also wondered if J.C. still received threatening messages. Brant could never get him to discuss it.

He decided to broach the subject lightly and see how Denice might feel about things.

"Have you said anything to J.C. about getting a Doberman?"

They had driven to one of the lakes in the area and were enjoying watching the intrepid sailboats enjoy one of the last days of warm weather before winter.

"Yes."

"What did he say?"

"Nothing." She looked at him with disgust. "He laughed."

"Did you explain that a Doberman was easier to train, more obedient and ate less than a husband?"

"Very funny. Sometimes I don't really believe Father takes me seriously."

"I know the feeling."

"Does he ever talk about the possibility of our marrying to you?" she asked.

"Nope."

"To me either. And Thanksgiving is only three weeks away. So I guess that means he's accepted that we aren't getting married."

"I wish I felt so secure in the knowledge."

"What do you mean?"

"I've just never seen J.C. back down on anything since I've known him."

"But this is different. I'm his daughter."

"Has he said anything more about the threatening notes?"

"Not a word."

"There is something else I've been meaning to ask you—"

She looked at him, waiting.

"Have you noticed how much weight your father has lost?"

She beamed. "Yes. Isn't it wonderful? I'm really proud of him."

"Proud?"

"Yes. He needed to lose weight."

"That's probably true. You don't think there's anything else wrong with him, do you?"

"With Father? Of course not. That man will live to be a hundred, you can count on that."

Brant discovered that he hoped he would. As tough as the old bird was, he had learned to admire him as well. He hated to think about all that dynamic energy and stamina disappearing. With a great deal of surprise, Brant realized he would miss him.

He hated to think what Denice would do.

After spending the past several weeks with her, Brant felt as though he knew Denice well. She was fairly uncomplicated, warm, outgoing and very loving.

It was her loving disposition that had created some awkward moments for him.

The more he was around her, the more he wanted to make love to her. After all, she was a very attractive woman, and since he'd been seeing her, he'd seen no one else.

He also knew that she knew next to nothing about lovemaking and didn't even seem to be aware of what she did to him when she melted in his arms and returned his kisses with enthusiasm. Denice was a warm and loving woman and would make some man a wonderful wife. Just not him.

He hoped J.C. had accepted that by now.

"What are you thinking?" Denice asked, and Brant realized they had been silent for some time.

"About you . . . and me, I suppose."

"What about us?"

"I'm not sure. We've been spending considerable time together, haven't we?"

"I suppose."

"Which plays right into your father's hands, doesn't it?"

"Not necessarily. A friendship such as ours certainly doesn't have to lead to marriage."

"Of course not." He was quiet for a moment. "You know, Denice, I want you to know how much I've enjoyed getting to know you. It's been a real revelation to me."

"In what way?"

"It's hard to explain. My life has been so different from yours. I never had what could be considered a normal family life. The women I've met have been a different breed from you. You're so soft, so vulnerable."

"Isn't everyone?"

"No. Not if they want to survive. Sometimes I wonder about you and how you're going to survive if something happens to J.C."

"I'll make it. You needn't worry about me."

"Glad to hear it. That certainly takes care of any niggling little doubts I might have had."

She laughed at his motion of dusting his hands.

"This world wasn't made for people like you," he added in a more serious tone. "You have to be strong to survive."

"I might surprise you, Brant. I'm stronger than I look."

"I hope so." He took her hand, and they started back to the car.

Denice invited Brant to stay for dinner that night, and they walked into the house laughing. J.C. stood in the hallway, watching them come through the door.

"Hello, Father. You're looking quite pleased with yourself. What have you been up to?" She walked over to J.C. and hugged him.

"I'm just enjoying seeing how well you two get along together, that's all."

Denice glanced over her shoulder at Brant. He watched the other two with a wary expression.

"Brant and I are friends, Father."

"That's a great way to have a relationship, daughter. I couldn't be more pleased."

"But that's all we are, Father. No matter what you think or hope."

He nodded. "We'll see."

She shook her head. "You are the most stubborn, opinionated man I've ever known. You never know when to give up."

"Thank you, my dear. I appreciate your words of encouragement."

Denice threw up her hands and started for the stairs. "I'll see you two later. I'm going to freshen up a little."

J.C. waved Brant into the study and poured him a glass of Scotch without asking. Handing it to him, he took the chair across from Brant and smiled.

"I want you to know that I'm proud of you. You've done an excellent job of courting her. An excellent job."

Since Brant had just taken a sip of Scotch those words almost caused him to choke.

"Courting her! I haven't been courting her."

"What would you call it?"

"Well, we've just been spending some of our free time together. It's all been very casual."

"Smart tactics. Give her plenty of space. Let her get to know you and feel comfortable with you. I couldn't have planned it any better myself."

"Dammit, J.C. I wish you'd get it out of your head that Denice and I are going to get married."

J.C. took a swallow from his drink and smiled.

The door to the hallway suddenly crashed against the wall, and Denice came storming into the room.

"What is the meaning of this!" Her voice was pitched lower than Brant had ever heard it, but he knew that she was angrier than he'd ever seen her.

Her father glanced up at her. "Ah, I see you've found your dress."

"Where did it come from?"

"I had it specially ordered from France. What do you think?"

"I think you have just wasted a great deal of money. I hope they'll allow you to return it."

"Why should I want to do that? After you've used it, I'm sure you'll want to keep it for your daughter's wedding someday."

Denice spun around and glared at Brant. "Did you know anything about this?"

"I don't have the faintest idea what you're talking about."

"I am talking about the wedding dress that is currently displayed on my bed upstairs, complete with veil, gloves and shoes."

Brant felt a definite sinking sensation. J. C. Roberts was living up to his reputation as a formidable opponent.

J.C. spoke. "I would suggest that you model it for us, but I understand it's bad luck for the groom to see his bride in her gown before the wedding."

"Father," Denice said in firm tones, "this is not a joke. You know very well I have no intention of marrying Brant, nor does he intend to marry me. I wish you would get that through your head."

J.C. studied the end of his glowing cigar. "The wedding invitations went out in yesterday's mail. The ballroom at The Hotel Crescent Court has been reserved for the reception, the floral decorations are ordered for the church. I wasn't sure which of your friends you wanted to have in the wedding, so I've arranged to have dresses made for whomever you choose, as well as their travel expenses taken care of."

She stared at him as though certain he would begin foaming at the mouth any moment. Denice slowly sank down on the sofa. "You can't be serious," she finally murmured, her face white.

"I would never joke about anything so important, my dear," J.C. calmly stated.

Denice's gaze slowly swung to Brant. "Did you know about any of this?"

He shook his head.

She continued to stare at Brant, ignoring his response. "You've known all along, haven't you? That's why you've spent time with me, been friends. You've been going through the softening-up process, so that I would be ready to fall into your arms by Thanksgiving." She looked at her father. "The two of you have been planning all of this for weeks, haven't you? And I've been so gullible that I fell right into your hands without a hint of a struggle."

"I know you're upset, Denice," Brant began.

"You are damn right about that, Mr. Malone. But that shouldn't bother you at all. You know how to get around that, don't you? You turn on that charm, smile at me and use those beautiful black eyes so well, and expect me to tumble into your arms."

She stood up and faced both of them. "Well, I won't do it, do you understand me? I will not marry you. I will not be forced into a situation such as this." She turned to her father. "All these years I thought you loved me and wanted the best for me, but all you've ever wanted was someone biddable to move around on your giant chessboard."

Denice started for the door, then paused. She turned around and looked at both men. "The Doberman is a much better idea."

She closed the door behind her.

Brant looked at Denice's father. J.C. took a sip of his bourbon, then looked over at Brant. He began to smile. "Beautiful black eyes, huh?" He began to chuckle.

"She'd prefer a Doberman, would she?" His chuckles turned into laughter. "Oh, but I love that gal of mine. She's something else, isn't she?"

"She isn't going to go through with it, J.C."

J.C. wiped his eyes. "Is that what you think? It's obvious you don't know much about women, Brant. At least not women like Denice. The lady doth protest too much, or didn't you notice?"

"I see nothing funny about manipulating people's lives, J.C. Nothing at all."

J.C. became serious. "I know you don't. That's one of the things that impresses me about you, Brant. You see people at a different level than I do. And it's surprising, considering the kind of life you've led. You care about people."

Brant continued to watch him without speaking.

"I've noticed your concern over me and my health, about your secretary's grandson, about the parking attendant's arthritis, about Denice and what's going to happen to her when I'm gone. It's something to think about."

"Yes, it is."

"But there's no reason to make her face that, just yet. As a matter of fact, that would only make her more stubborn. I want her to begin building her own life...with you."

Brant got up and walked over to the fireplace. Staring down at the flames, he rested his elbow on the mantel. "J.C., you need to understand something about me, something I'm sure you haven't given much thought. It's true I care for people. I'm interested in them, and will help them if I can. But I don't love them and I don't want them to love me. I don't want that sort of a relationship."

He looked at J.C. "Denice deserves more than I can give her. More than I am capable of giving her. Don't do this to her."

"Don't underestimate yourself, Brant. Give it a chance. There's no time limit set. Take each day as it comes. You've done that at the office and have managed to work some damn miracles. You've already made a difference in Denice's life. Why do you think she's so upset?"

"What do you mean?"

"Her biggest concern, although granted she hasn't faced it yet, is that you are being forced to marry *her*, not the other way around. It's her pride that's talking now, that's all. Just her pride." He smiled. "If you were to admit that you loved her and wanted to marry her, she'd change her tune quicker than a flash."

"But I don't love her. And I don't want to marry her."

"Well, son, that's a real shame. Because that's exactly what you're going to do . . . the day after Thanksgiving."

Seven

The church, one of the largest in the city, overflowed with people who not only wanted to see the wedding of the year, the wedding of the daughter of Jefferson Calhoun Roberts, but wanted to be seen as one of the fortunate ones who had received an invitation.

No one thought much about receiving an invitation to a wedding only a couple of weeks in advance. After all, this was Texas, and Texas abounded with eccentrics. J. C. Roberts reigned high on the list of eccentrics. No one cared to predict what he would do next.

A surprisingly large number of people were amazed to know he even *had* a daughter, so there were many who came out of curiosity. Why had so few people heard of her? She had never been brought out in society, at least

not in Texas society. And she'd never had her picture in
the *Dallas Morning News*.

What was wrong with her?

Speculation had her as horribly disfigured, crippled or
mentally deficient. The patients and personnel of the
children's hospital had never associated the Denice they
knew with J. C. Roberts. Roberts was, after all, a fairly
common name.

Absolutely no one had ever heard of the bridegroom.

When J.C. walked into the small room that held the
bride and her attendants, school friends who had oblig-
ingly flown to Texas to participate in the day, he found it
difficult to catch his breath.

Never had he seen his daughter look more beautiful.
She stood by the window, staring out at the cool, rather
blustery view, the sun doing its best to warm the day for
her. She looked as though she belonged on top of a giant
wedding cake: Denice was the epitome of the traditional
bride, the satin of her dress looking no smoother than her
creamy complexion, the lace no more delicate than her
features.

Her hair glowed against the white lace of her veil, the
sun touching it through the glass window, creating a golden aureole around her head.

When her attendants saw him, they took his presence
to be a signal that it was time to go. With last-minute hugs
and best wishes, they scampered through the door to take
their places.

Denice had not looked at him since he'd come into the
room.

"I wish your mother could see you," he said, his voice
gruff.

She looked past him. "Is it time to go?"

"We have a few minutes yet. Denice, don't you think you've carried this grudge long enough?"

His comment had the desired effect. Her gaze met his. Her eyes glowed with an inner fire, a sparkle like he'd never seen before. If he had ever wondered if his daughter had inherited anything from him, he knew she had—his temper.

Her anger had been cold—then fiery. Always fierce. She had stated her position calmly, later lost her temper and shouted. She had raged and stormed, pleaded and begged. When she'd faced that she was up against a person who had spent his life mastering the art of manipulating people, she had finally bowed her head and accepted the inevitable.

Since that time Denice had not spoken of the matter to her father again. As a matter of fact, she hadn't spoken to him at all.

She looked at the man before her in his cutaway coat and tails, his heavily starched shirt, his impeccably knotted tie and said, "Grudge, J.C.? Is that what you think this is?" She smiled, but it wasn't a pleasant smile. "I shall never forget what you have done. Never." Her voice was hollow and toneless, which gave her words more depth and meaning than if she had yelled them at him.

"Honey, don't be this way. Today is your wedding day. The most wonderful day of a young woman's life. I want you to enjoy it, be happy."

"With my bought and paid for bridegroom? Sorry, J.C. I would have much preferred to have found and purchased my own."

"Quit calling me J.C., dammit!"

"Whatever you say. You make the rules. I just live by them."

One of the girls poked her head around the door. "It's time to go, you two."

The older man and the young woman stood facing each other, the man confronted with the consequences of his own actions, the woman hurting so deep inside she wasn't sure the pain would ever go away.

"You have sacrificed the relationship we've shared for the past twenty-four years for your own mysterious reasons. I hope they were worth it." Her voice was a hoarse whisper.

The pain in Denice's eyes seemed to pierce him. She was right. Nothing would ever be the same between them again. J.C. nodded slowly, acknowledging her view of the situation. There wasn't much else he could do. He held out his arm to her, and she took it, lifting her gown slightly as they walked out the door and prepared to go down the aisle.

Brant had never been in clothes so formal before, and he felt like a complete fool. He had known no one to ask to be his best man, so the husband of the matron of honor had volunteered to perform those duties and had come to get him when it was time to go to the altar.

The size of the crowd had shocked him when he'd stepped through the doorway at the front of the church. The sudden quiet at his entrance, then the whispered comments behind gloved hands, had irritated him. Hadn't they ever seen anyone dressed like that before?

Now his eyes quickly scanned the crowd. He didn't know a person there. No one from the company had been invited. Only top-drawer dignitaries and socialites had made the list.

He was the only one there who didn't belong.

He suddenly thought about Jake, the old man who'd taken in a hungry ten-year-old boy, and tried to picture him sitting there waiting for the circus to begin. The thought amused him, and he relaxed slightly, a smile hovering on his mouth.

"God, he's gorgeous, Cindy. Would you look at those shoulders? He could put his shoes under my bed anytime."

Brant heard the whisper and the sound of someone hushing the speaker somewhere on his left. He kept his eyes trained on the back of the room, watching as each attendant came slowly, with small measured steps, toward him.

Then the music changed, and the crowd stood up. J.C. and Denice started down the aisle.

Brant had not seen Denice since the day she had found her wedding gown waiting for her. For the past few weeks he had gone about his work, waiting for J.C. to tell him to go back to the field and that the wedding was canceled. He had done neither.

Instead he'd taken Brant to be fitted for formal wear, shown him the church where he was going to be married, asked if he had anyone he wanted to invite and, on the day before Thanksgiving, told Brant when to be at the church.

Brant hadn't been surprised at Denice's lack of success. He had yet to meet anyone who could change J. C. Roberts's mind after it had been made up.

Although it was eleven in the morning, the church was lit with candles that scented the spacious area. White roses adorned each pew, and large stands of them covered the altar of the church.

Yet all of the people, the flowers, the candles and the music disappeared when Brant saw Denice coming toward him on her father's arm.

She looked like something from a fairy tale—her dress so full that she could scarcely walk down the wide aisle without brushing against the rows of pews. Her waist looked so tiny that he wondered if his hands would reach around it, and he was suddenly reminded of the day he had lifted her off her horse and brought her body close to his.

Her veil framed her face but did not hide it, and when she reached him he studied the porcelain paleness of her face, noticing for the first time a light dusting of freckles over her nose.

Her lack of color worried him, and when she placed her hand in his as instructed by the minister, Brant grew even more concerned at its coldness. He had to stop himself from chafing her hands to get some warmth into them.

Denice had steeled herself to go through with the farce of a ceremony, refusing to think about what her father had managed to accomplish because of her love for him. Since she had never opposed him in her life, he had assumed that he could use her to fulfill whatever mysterious plans he had made. She had not been prepared for such an overt move to mold her into a life of his choosing.

Now he was going to marry her off to a man who he felt was enough like him to take his place, both in the business and at home.

Her first glimpse of Brant caused her to forget the cadence of the slow march. In the formal wedding clothes he looked sensational. For whatever his reason for choosing to wear it, black was definitely his color. The white ruffled shirt made his tanned skin look almost bronze in color. His hair lay perfectly groomed and shaped on his well-formed head. He stood watching her as she approached him as though she were the most important person in the world to him.

She almost faltered when his gaze met hers. The black gleam seemed to possess her in some way that she found almost pleasurable—as though his protection of her began immediately and no one would ever touch her. Except him.

The thought of him touching her caused a shiver to course through her, and when she placed her hand into his large warm one once again, she felt a sense of homecoming, of being safe.

Denice tried to concentrate on the words of the service, tried not to be so conscious of the tall man who stood so solemnly by her side, tried not to notice the slight scent of his after-shave that reminded her of the friend who had shared so much of his time with her these past several weeks. The traitorous friend.

The minister murmured the words, "You may kiss the bride," and Brant turned to her, lifting her chin slightly with his forefinger. Slowly he bent toward her, his gaze never leaving hers. At the last moment her eyes fluttered closed and she felt his warm lips press against hers in a mere promise of a kiss. Then they were gone.

Denice never clearly recalled the rest of that day. They rode to The Hotel Crescent Court in silence. The food and champagne seemed never-ending. There was a brief moment of clarity when she and Brant cut the cake together, the photographer duly snapping pictures. Brant seldom smiled during any of it. Denice missed the companion with the devilish grin and unexpected flashing smile.

At one point he leaned over and asked softly, "Are you holding up all right? Would you like to leave?"

She was surprised at his concern. At the moment nothing sounded better than to get away from all the noise and confusion, the happy voices and ribald comments, to some quiet place. But it was another two hours before they managed to get away.

He had parked his car at the hotel the night before, taking a taxi to the church. They had ridden to the hotel in her father's limousine, with Harris driving as usual. Now they could go.

Brant bundled her into the small car, stuffing yards of satin in behind her until the absurdity of it all struck her and she began to laugh. After finally managing to get the door closed, Brant slid into the driver's seat and said, "Hello? Is there anyone there under all that material?" He started the car, and they pulled away, heading north out of town.

"I can hardly breathe," Denice managed to complain, patting down her dress so she could see. She glanced out the window. "Where are we going?"

"I thought you'd want to go home," he said quietly.

"Yes, I would," she answered him in the same tone.

They rode for several miles in silence. Finally Brant said, "Since I wasn't sure whether there would actually be a wedding, I didn't make plans to take you anywhere on a honeymoon."

Her golden-eyed gaze met his briefly before he looked back at the road. "Surely there was no doubt in your mind that J.C. would prevail, was there?" she asked.

"You're a pretty strong-willed person yourself, you know."

"Me? Hardly. I married you, didn't I?"

"Yes, because you didn't want to destroy the relationship the two of you share."

"He's already destroyed it."

"No, he hasn't. I think he's been afraid that he pushed you too far, that you would leave him, move out and find a place of your own and make your own way. We both know you could have done that."

She stared out the window for a long while without speaking, then sighed. "I know. I almost did, but when it came right down to it, I couldn't leave him." She looked at Brant a little helplessly. "I'm all he has."

"Very few men are ever lucky enough to know that sort of love and loyalty. Your father is a very fortunate man."

They were silent the rest of the way to her home.

The house seemed so silent somehow, and Denice realized that she had become accustomed to the noise at the reception. Morton informed them that J.C. would not be home until later and that dinner would be served at six.

Denice groaned. "I couldn't eat another thing." She started up the stairway, lifting her skirt and petticoats.

Brant stood in the foyer watching her for a moment before he said, "Are you going to need any help getting out of that thing?"

She glanced down at him in surprise. She hadn't even thought about it, but it had taken two of her attendants to help her get into it. Was *he* offering to help her? she wondered a little uncertainly. A rueful smile appeared on her face. "I suppose I am. This dress was definitely designed for a lady's maid."

He started up the stairway behind her. "I haven't had that much experience, but I'm willing to help." The slight smile he gave her made her catch her breath. There was nothing threatening or sinister about his look, nor for that matter, lecherous. If anything, his smile indicated he was poking fun at himself, playing lady's maid to his new bride, a woman who hadn't wanted to marry him.

Brant followed her into her suite of rooms, looking around with interest. "I had no idea you had so much room to yourself."

"Yes. Actually this is a fully self-contained apartment, but I never bother eating up here. Father needed the company." She didn't notice—and he didn't point out to her—that she had slipped back into the easy familiarity of using her special name for her parent.

She showed him her bedroom, a room that actually took up one side of the house, from front to back, so that three sides had windows. A massive bed was against the fourth wall, with a dressing room and bath hinted at through an open door near the bed.

Turning her back on him and pointing to the tiny buttons going down the back of the dress, Denice tried to explain what she was feeling. "I never pretended that I wanted to get married," she began somewhat hesitantly.

"That's true," he agreed with a slight smile.

She felt his hands brushing against her back as he worked his way down her spine, and she wished he didn't have to stand so close. She could smell his after-shave, and found herself distracted by its evocative scent.

"It isn't as though we're in love or anything," she said, her voice quivering slightly.

Brant grinned at her nervousness but said nothing. He found the unimpeded view of her spine interesting enough. He let her talk.

"So I knew you'd understand why I had Morton place another bed over there in the alcove for you."

Brant jerked his head up. "You did what?"

She pointed over into a corner that he hadn't previously noticed. Sure enough, there was a single bed made up and waiting.

He began to laugh.

"What's so funny?" she asked suspiciously.

"You are."

"In what way?" she asked stiffly.

He finished unbuttoning the dress and walked around in front of her, a light dancing in his eyes that she found most attractive. She clutched the front of the dress to her and waited.

"You might at least have waited to be asked before turning me down." He moved toward the door. "I'm going back to town. I've got to pack and close my apartment, now that I'm a happily married man. I'll see you later."

Denice stood in the middle of her spacious bedroom, clutching her wedding gown to her breasts, feeling as though she'd made a terrible mistake. And it wasn't because she had married Brant Malone.

Eight

Denice told Morton to hold dinner until Brant returned. She saw no point in her sitting there eating alone when she wasn't even hungry.

What a bewildering wedding day it had been. Nothing about her wedding had been what she'd expected. Everyone had seemed happy for her, and Brant had watched over her with a naturalness that seemed inherent to his nature. She felt so confused. He had become a close friend, and now the friendship was ruined. She was surprised he wasn't showing his irritation at being forced to marry her. Would she ever understand him?

It seemed strange to think they were married. She was now Mrs. Brant Malone. Denice Roberts Malone. So much for trying to live her own life, make her own destiny, be the captain of her ship, the master of her soul.

She had just married the man her father had chosen for her to marry.

But not without a struggle. For some reason that was important to her. She might have lost the war, but she had certainly engaged in a few strong battles. Had she gained anything out of the experience?

She had discovered something about herself that had really unnerved her when she'd seen Brant waiting for her at the end of the aisle. If her father had chosen for her to marry any other man than Brant Malone, she would have packed her bags, moved out and never looked back.

She needed to come to terms with her own feelings. She liked him. The more she got to know him, got past that shield that seemed to be an integral part of him, the more she enjoyed him. Denice had been willing to accept what he was willing to offer—friendship. How could she live with the fact that he had been forced to give her more?

Feeling the strain of the day, Denice decided to take a nap. After giving Morton instructions regarding dinner, she went back upstairs and curled up on her bed with her comforter tucked cozily around her. She fell deeply asleep and didn't wake up until her bedroom door opened.

She sat up in bed, disoriented. A lamp came on, and she saw Brant standing in the bedroom doorway, a suitcase in his hand.

"Don't you believe in knocking?" she asked a little querulously.

His left brow lifted slightly. "I thought this was my room," he said in a polite voice.

"Well, it is. I mean—"

"I'm not in the habit of knocking on my own door." He stood there looking at her with an amused expression. He walked into the room, set the suitcase down and began to unbutton his shirt.

"What are you doing?" she asked, sliding off the bed and staring at him.

"What does it look like I'm doing?"

"Getting undressed!"

"Very good. It's reassuring to know that your father didn't waste his money on your education. You've developed good deductive and reasoning processes."

He unfastened his belt and sat down on the side of the bed.

"But you can't. I mean—why are you getting undressed?"

After removing his socks and shoes, he stood again and looked at her. "Are we going to go through this question-and-answer routine every time I take a shower? Wouldn't it be better to leave a little of the mystery in our relationship? Or are you going to insist on my explaining everything I do to you."

"A shower." She could feel her face heating up. "Oh."

He stepped out of his pants unconcernedly. "Or did you want to use the shower first?" he asked.

"Uh, no, that's all right. You go ahead," she said in her polished finishing-school voice.

He chuckled. "Thank you." He went into the bathroom and shut the door.

Denice slowly sank to the side of the bed. Why hadn't she thought of this? Not only would they be sharing a room, but a bathroom as well. She could dress in privacy if she wished, but it was obvious he wasn't going to be concerned about modesty, either hers or his.

He looked bigger somehow with his clothes off. She had tried to keep her eyes away from him until he'd left the room but the fleeting glimpses she had gotten had affected her in strange ways. She seemed to have forgotten how to breathe in the normal, everyday fashion, and her heart had begun acrobatic stunts in her chest.

She wasn't a prude. A physical therapist was very much at home with the human anatomy. But she'd never had a male anatomy sharing her bedroom before. It would take some getting used to.

Denice was even less prepared for the sight of Brant coming out of the bathroom briskly toweling his hair while another towel hung low around his hips. She caught herself twisting her fingers together while she stood watching him. Had she lost her mind? She walked over to her dresser and picked up a brush, flicking it rapidly through her hair.

She watched him through the mirror as he casually picked up his suitcase and opened it on her bed. He glanced up suddenly and caught her eye.

"Where can I put my things?"

Dropping her hairbrush, she jerkily pulled open the top left drawer of the double dresser. "You can have this set of drawers if you'd like." She walked into the dressing area and pointed. "And you can use that wall to hang up your clothes."

"I don't have all that much to hang up, but thanks."

She watched him as he methodically unpacked. He placed things neatly in the drawers and hung up his shirts and pants.

"You only have one suit?"

"Yes."

"Do you intend to buy more?"

"I haven't given it much thought. Why?"

"Well, because, you, uh, well, you're the head of the company and—"

"And suits are standard uniform?"

"Something like that."

"Then I'll have to stay out of uniform."

"You prefer to dress in black."

"You got it."

Forcing herself to keep her eyes on his face, she had almost gotten used to his near nudity and was gradually relaxing. Then he dropped the towel from around his waist, reached into one of the drawers for a pair of briefs and calmly stepped into them as though he were alone.

Denice caught a glimpse of her face in the mirror. She looked like a sunburn victim, her face was so fiery red. Almost running to the door, she said over her shoulder, "I'll see you downstairs for dinner."

"More than likely," he agreed, watching the door close behind her.

So Miss Roberts—oops, make that Mrs. Malone— wasn't used to male nudity. He found that a little hard to believe, considering her occupation. Perhaps it was *his* male nudity that was causing her distress.

Denice found dinner conversation difficult. She searched for something to say. During the past several weeks she'd grown accustomed to Brant's tendency toward silence. She couldn't understand why it made her nervous tonight.

"Did you get everything packed today?" she asked in a desperate effort to relieve the silence between them.

Brant glanced up from his plate. His penetrating gaze took in her flushed cheeks, her slightly tilted nose with its tiny crown of freckles and her very kissable mouth. His eyes lingered on her lips when he answered.

"Yes. There wasn't much to pack."

"You must not be a collector if you travel that light."

"That's true."

She leaned her chin on her hand and gazed at him. "I know so little about you. During the weeks since we met you've learned everything about me—from the name of my second grade teacher to the fellow who first stole my heart in the eighth grade."

He smiled the slow intimate smile she found so attractive and said, "There are still a few things I haven't learned about you."

The look that accompanied his words left little doubt in her mind what he was thinking about.

Denice couldn't think of anything to say for the rest of the meal.

"Would you like coffee now?" Morton asked after their plates had been removed.

Denice glanced at Brant. He shook his head and stood up. "Not now, thank you. I think I'll go talk with the security people and get acquainted with how things are being handled around here." He touched her lightly on the tip of her nose with his finger and winked. "I'll see you later, Mrs. Malone."

Bemused, Denice watched him walk out of the room.

"Will that be all, Miss Denice?"

She started, suddenly aware she was still sitting in her chair, staring at the doorway where Brant had disappeared. "Uh, yes, Morton. That will be all."

She wandered back upstairs, turned on the television, watched five minutes each of three different shows, turned off the television, picked up a book, read one page four times and had no idea what the book was about, dropped the book and walked over to the window.

Denice tried to think of what she would be doing if this was an ordinary evening in her life, but her mind wasn't that easily fooled. It was not an ordinary evening. It was her wedding night.

Not that it made any difference to her. Brant knew very well where she stood. They didn't have a normal sort of relationship. He wouldn't expect her to sleep with him. Or would he? Surely not so soon, anyway.

Ah-hah. I caught that. You're already wondering when you're going to sleep with him!

"I am not."

You're wondering what he's like in bed.

"I am not!"

You're even wondering if he wants to make love to you.

"I am not!"

"Are you having some sort of one-sided argument with yourself?" he asked, coming into the room. "Who's doing the 'I ams'?"

She spun around and glared at him. "Must you sneak in here like that?"

Brant spread his hands out in supplication. "I wasn't sneaking anywhere. I just walked in and found you talking to yourself." He walked over to the television. "Anything worth watching on television?"

"I don't know."

"Oh. I suppose television isn't intellectual enough for you?"

"Why would you say that?"

"Oh, it's probably all of that polish and pizzazz you carry around."

"Why do I get the feeling you're making fun of me?"

"Not me, honey. Listen, I'm impressed as hell with you and your education. I was lucky to finish high school."

"Does that bother you?"

He had brought a bottle of Scotch up with him, along with a glass containing some ice, sat down, stretched his legs out in front of him and crossed them at the ankles. He leaned his head against the back of the chair and looked up at her, his face serious. "Yeah, I guess it does."

"You could always go back to school if you wished."

"Don't have the patience for it. The kind of schooling I got doesn't come with a diploma."

She sat down in the chair across from him. "Brant, won't you please tell me a little about yourself?"

"Sorry. I'm not interested in the interview, ma'am. I already got the job."

"Why are you being so rude?"

"Why are you being so nosy?"

"Because I want to get to know you."

"Why?"

"Surely that's obvious. Because you're my husband."

He took a drink of Scotch and let it slowly trickle down his throat. The more he thought about it, the more he liked the idea of just sitting there and quietly getting drunk. What better way to celebrate a wedding night?

He rolled his head slowly against the back of the chair until he was looking at her. "So I am. What do you think I should do about it?"

"I'm not sure I understand what you mean."

"Of course you do. I am now married to a beautiful woman who has made it quite clear she doesn't want me in her bed. Do I lie down and play dead like a good watchdog or do what I want to do?"

Denice's hand restlessly picked at the hem of her skirt where it lay against her crossed knee. She tried to keep her eyes on him, but she couldn't. "What do you want to do?" she managed to say.

Brant finished off his drink, picked up the bottle and filled the glass again. "Now there's a good question. I believe I'll drink to that one." He raised his glass once more, then looked back at Denice, fascinated by the way the soft light from the lamp fell on her burnished waves.

He started to speak in his low, husky voice, the words slowly circling and surrounding her with their sound and meaning, hypnotizing her.

"I'd like to pick you up in my arms and carry you through that door over there that leads to your spacious bedroom. I'd like to put you on the bed, unfasten your dress and slip it over your head, leaving you in your lacy little slip and undies. I'd like to slip your shoes off and start kissing you from the arch of your dainty foot to that flirtatious little dimple in your cheek until I've kissed every inch of your body."

He slowly closed his eyes while he continued to speak. "I'd like to show you what it means to be a wife in the fullest sense of the word. I'd like to teach you what to do to please me, show you your own sensual nature and free the woman that has been hidden away in that virginal body of yours all of these years."

His eyes snapped open, and he stared at her without expression. "That's what I'd like to do." He stood up suddenly. "But instead of that I'm going to go to bed." He walked across the room to the bedroom door. "Good night." He stepped into the other room, paused and looked back over his shoulder at her. "Pleasant dreams."

Denice sat there staring at the door in shocked disbelief. She felt as though Brant had done all of those things to her. Her body tingled every place he had mentioned, from the arch of her foot to the dimple in her cheek.

"Damn him!"

It was too early for bed. She decided to go downstairs and find a book to read.

Two hours later she began to yawn and discovered it was almost midnight. No wonder she was tired. She hadn't heard her father come in. Maybe he'd decided to stay downtown. With considerable reluctance Denice went upstairs. She needn't have worried. Brant was sound asleep. No doubt the two double Scotches he had downed had contributed to his rest.

She went into the bathroom to undress, turned out the light and felt her way to bed. Within minutes, she, too, was asleep.

Sometime during the course of the night a cold, wet norther blew in. Brant woke up shivering. His bed had only one blanket, and because he was by the windows, he could feel the cold.

He crawled out of bed and went into the dressing room. There were no extra blankets. He checked everywhere he could think of. There were no chests or closets in the room. Shrugging, he walked back into the bedroom and looked at his beautiful wife curled up so comfortably beneath a pile of blankets. He thought about it for a moment, then shrugged.

With any luck he'd be awake and gone before she stirred. He'd have to ask Morton for more blankets tomorrow. In the meantime—

He crawled into the warm bed and promptly fell back to sleep.

Denice's dream seemed to fulfill all of her secret longings. She swept down a long aisle toward the man of her dreams who greeted her with open arms, lifting her high above his head and swinging her around. Then the aisle was gone and they were in a field of bluebonnets with horses grazing nearby, and he was kissing her, kissing her, kissing her.

She floated along in a sensual haze of satisfaction and fulfillment, held close in his arms.

Held close in his arms?

Denice's eyes flew open. The windows were only slightly lighter than the room. Night still held but dawn approached. She lay on her side, her back snuggled against a hard, warm body. Knees were drawn up under hers, and a muscular arm was wrapped around her waist, holding her close. Gingerly she turned her head. Brant slept soundly beside her.

She should have felt outrage. Instead, she almost laughed. The room was much cooler than it had been the night before. The unpredictable Texas weather must have taken another sudden turn. Brant's bed had a blanket and a spread on it, which would have been enough in the mild weather. Obviously it wasn't enough now.

Denice considered her options, but she was too comfortable to go find more blankets. She just couldn't really work up much enthusiasm about moving at all. She closed her eyes and smiled. Maybe she would dream again, she hoped as she drifted off to sleep once more.

A few hours Brant woke up disoriented and with his head pounding. Where the hell was he? He glanced at the tousled head next to him. And who the hell with?

He sat up and stared around the room. The sight of the bed in the alcove across from him jogged his memory. He groaned.

What a way to start off the relationship, showing her he couldn't be trusted to stay away from her. He eased out of bed and headed for the shower, hoping Morton would have coffee made by the time he got downstairs.

Fifteen minutes later he walked into the dining room and found J.C. sitting there, reading the paper and drinking coffee. He looked surprised to see Brant.

"You're up a little early, aren't you?"

"I get up around this time every morning."

"Well, I thought maybe you'd make an exception this morning."

"Why should I?"

"Beats the hell out of me. Maybe I'm older than I thought, but unless my memory has completely gone haywire, newlyweds spend a great deal of time in bed together for the first few weeks."

Brant smiled and took a sip of his coffee with evident pleasure. "I suppose real newlyweds would, but Denice and I don't have that sort of marriage, as you well know."

J.C. put down his coffee cup and stared suspiciously at the man across from him. "No, as a matter of fact, I don't know."

"Well, you should. You're the one who arranged it. You wanted me here as her watchdog. That's what I am."

"Of course I want you here to protect her—which means you need to be right there with her every night."

"I am. She had a bed set up not thirty feet away from hers. Nothing could possibly disturb her without my knowing about it."

"Another bed! What the hell did she mean putting in another bed?"

"I believe your daughter is making a statement about who she is and her right to lead her own life. Personally, I respect the hell out of her for it."

"And you don't even mind?"

Brant shrugged. "Sleeping with her wasn't part of the deal. If you wanted stud service, you should have explained more clearly."

"Stud service! Listen, Malone, that's my daughter you're talking about and I don't appreciate—"

"Neither does she. That's why she had another bed put in the room."

Morton came in with several steaming dishes.

"Good morning, Morton," Brant said with a smile. "You must have known I was hungry." He filled his plate and handed a dish to J.C. "Aren't you eating?"

J.C. looked at all the food and remembered his diet. He had actually lost several pounds in the weeks he'd been on it, and he wasn't going to be lured off of it now. Stud service, indeed. His own daughter!

"I have to watch what I eat," he finally muttered.

Brant paused, his fork in midair. How could he have forgotten the reason J.C. had felt the need to blackmail him into marrying his daughter?

"I think you should get a second opinion."

J.C. was still upset over the news of two beds in Denice's room, and he growled, "About what?"

"Your health."

"I know the exact condition of my health. I don't need any more opinions, thank you."

"You mean there's nothing anyone can do?"

"We'll see," he muttered.

"I'm glad I had a chance to see you before Denice comes down. We need to talk about these threats you've been receiving."

"They're being taken care of. You needn't worry about it."

"But that's part of my job here, to worry about it."

"The hell it is. I just want you to take care of Denice. You let me worry about the rest of it."

Brant shrugged. "She doesn't need taking care of."

"That's what you think. That may even be what she thinks. But I know better. And I'm going to be proved right yet, you just wait and see. I know human nature better than either of you."

Brant stared at the older man, puzzled at his vehemence. Then he continued to eat his breakfast in silence.

Nine

———

Morton had removed Brant's plate and was pouring him another cup of coffee when Denice walked into the dining room. Brant watched her warily, unsure of whether she knew he had shared her bed and blankets the night before.

J.C. dropped the paper he'd been reading and watched her take a seat at the table.

Denice gave nothing of her thoughts away. She glanced at each of the men, murmured "Good morning," then smiled at Morton as he poured coffee for her.

J.C. cleared his throat. "Did you sleep well?"

With calm deliberation Denice picked up her cup. "I slept very well, Father." She gave a sidelong glance at Brant. "In fact, I was toasty warm all night." She sipped from the cup in front of her. "I wasn't even aware the weather had changed until I woke up this morning."

Brant eyed her across his coffee cup. "No wonder you felt so warm," he drawled. "That flannel nightgown you sleep in must have ten yards in it, at least. It's more like a tent!"

J.C. studied the couple for a moment. "You mean you slept in a flannel nightgown on your wedding night?"

Her eyes met her father's gaze. "Of course. I always sleep in one during the winter."

"Your mother had no need of anything like that once we were married." He glowered at her.

Her expression didn't change. "I think the situation is considerably different, don't you, Father?" She tilted her head slightly. "Or did Grandfather buy you as a husband for his daughter, too?"

Both men choked slightly.

"That wasn't funny, Denice," J.C. finally muttered.

She eyed Brant in a speculative manner. "I must admit, though, you have excellent taste in men, Father. I really believe you got your money's worth!"

Brant slammed his cup down, shoved his chair back and strode out of the room.

Denice began to eat the breakfast Morton set before her.

"Was that really necessary?" her father finally asked.

She looked up at him in surprise. "Did I say something wrong?"

"Don't you care that you hurt Brant's feelings?"

"Feelings, Father? You have to have feelings before they can be hurt. I don't believe you have to worry about Brant in that respect."

"You're reading him wrong, you know. I thought you would be able to see what is inside him better than that. That man has been hurt—very badly. He carries some emotional scars that will never go away. So he's learned to protect himself."

"How do you know so much about him, Father? I can never get him to tell me anything about his past."

"He hasn't told me anything, either, but I have ways of finding out. I don't divulge sources and I don't repeat what I've learned. Perhaps someday he'll be willing to tell you, but not if you continue to make cheap shots like that one at him."

She stared down at her plate for a few moments, her appetite gone. "I wish I understood why he agreed to marry me."

"I gave him no choice. Or at least I thought so at the time. But now that I think about it the man I know him to be wouldn't have tolerated my threats. He would have told me to do my worst and be done with it. Instead, after a few minor kicks, he accepted the situation. I've been asking myself why, and I'm not sure I know the answer. He's deep, that one. Doesn't let anyone get close to him."

Denice stood up. "I don't suppose it really matters at this point, Father. You got what you wanted. Obviously, that's all that's important to you. How Brant or I manage to deal with the mess you've made of our lives is of little consequence to you."

She turned and walked out of the room.

J.C. sat there and stared after her. Yes, he had gotten what he wanted, but at what price? Had he lost his daughter because of his tactics? Only time would tell.

He felt his years weighing on him. He was forced to face the fact that personal relationships could not be handled in the same manner as business relationships. He hoped he hadn't made that discovery too late.

Denice felt ashamed of herself. She hadn't meant to be rude to Brant. None of the events surrounding their marriage was his fault. However, she was finding it increasingly difficult to be civil to her father. She would have to come to terms with the fact that he could ignore her feelings so completely. She had never seen the ruthless side of his character before. Obviously Brant had.

Once again she was forced to consider that Brant had been given little choice. So he had married her. There was no reason why she should continue to throw the circumstances of their marriage up to him. If nothing else, she would like to feel they could salvage the friendship they had begun to build.

The first thing she had to do was find Brant and apologize to him. After searching the house, she admitted to herself that finding him was going to be as difficult as offering the apology.

When she finally resorted to asking Morton if he knew where Brant had gone, Morton informed her that Brant had taken one of the horses out for a ride.

She glanced out the window and shivered. The wind blustered and swirled around the house and grounds. Low-hanging gray clouds scudded across the sky. Not a day she would have chosen to go riding, but if she wanted to see Brant in the near future, she didn't have much choice.

After calling down to the stables and asking for her horse to be saddled, Denice dressed as warmly as possible and ventured outside.

The air smelled fresh and clean, and she inhaled deeply. The moisture from the night before had released the fragrance of the soil as well as the odor of the wet grass and bushes, scenting the air with an earthy smell she found appealing.

The stable hand pointed her in the direction Brant had taken, and she began to follow the trail, thinking all the while about what she was going to say to him.

She came across him at the same clearing where they had stopped during their previous ride. He sat on the felled tree trunk, gazing off into the distance. The sound of her horse's hooves thudding on the rain-softened ground caused him to turn his head and watch her approach.

Denice stopped her mount near his and smiled at him. "Hi," she said with a tentative smile.

He nodded but said nothing.

She slid off her horse and dropped the reins over its head. "I hope I'm not intruding."

His mouth tightened slightly, and he shrugged. "On the contrary, I believe it's been made clear that I'm the intruder." He spoke evenly, without expression, as though it made no difference to him.

Sitting down beside him, she burst into speech. "Brant, I'm sorry for what I said. It was spiteful, hateful, and there was no excuse for my behavior. I was trying to hurt my father for his heavy-handedness in our affairs. Instead, I hurt you."

He had been watching the horizon while she spoke, but at her last words he turned his head and looked at her. "You didn't hurt me."

"All right. But I'm really ashamed of myself. I hope you'll forgive me."

After a moment he said, "There's really nothing to forgive. We both know I've been bought and paid for. There's no way I could keep you in the manner you're used to. I don't think I'd even want to try. This sort of life isn't for me."

"What sort of life?"

"Living behind high walls. Living in fear of threats. I came back to the States to find a quiet, peaceful existence where I could learn to trust people again."

"Instead, you got tangled up with the Roberts clan."

"Something like that."

"We could have the marriage annulled."

His laugh was dry and without humor. "That would really create a scandal for you."

"I wouldn't care, not if you want your freedom."

He shrugged. "I think I've come to accept that there is no such thing as freedom. It's a useful little word to wave around and comes in handy during election years. But none of us are ever free—free from our past, free from fear, free from our memories."

"Would it help if you shared some of those memories?"

He glanced at her, then away. "Not really."

"Well, then," she said in a brisk voice, "what do you suggest we do now?"

"About what?"

"Us."

"Is there an us?"

She forced herself to meet his black-eyed gaze. Her heart was beating so fast she was certain he could hear it. "I would like there to be," she said softly.

Something flashed in his eyes, an expression that came and went so quickly she couldn't identify it.

"I'm sorry I didn't have enough blankets on your bed last night," she said, hoping he would discuss the fact that he had shared her bed at least part of the night.

"Morton said he'd have more put on today," he responded noncommittally.

"Oh." So much for that. "Aren't you cold, sitting out here in the wind?"

He glanced up at the sky as though just then becoming aware of the wind and lowering sky. "Compared to Wyoming, this is just a frisky, mild breeze."

She shivered slightly.

"But you're cold, aren't you?"

"A little," she admitted.

He stood, pulling her up with him. "Why don't we go back and see if Morton will produce some hot chocolate for us?"

She nodded, unsure what to say.

He leaned over and kissed her softly on the lips. "Thank you for coming out here to find me. I appreciate it."

Lifting her, he placed her in the saddle, then leaped on his horse without help of the stirrup.

She laughed at his stunt. "Something tells me that isn't the first time you've done that."

He grinned, and she caught her breath. His smile strongly affected her. He looked years younger with his eyes dancing and the sudden flash of white from his smile contrasting with his tanned face. "Guess I was showing off a little."

"If I could do that, I'd be showing off all the time," she admitted with a wide grin.

His laugh sounded more relaxed than she had ever heard from him. "I'll race you," he said, nudging his horse in the flanks.

She leaned over her mount and shouted, "You're on!"

They raced all the way back. The horses were evenly matched, but his skill as a rider made the final difference, and he beat her by almost a length.

The horses had enjoyed it almost as much as the riders and were ready to continue the contest. Denice laughingly protested and suggested the stable hands might want to continue with their exercise.

Brant dropped his arm companionably around her shoulders, and they walked into the house together.

Married life seemed to make few changes in Denice's routine. As the days became weeks, she continued to spend her days at the hospital, trying to adjust to the idea that she was now married.

Brant made no demands on her. On the contrary, she scarcely knew he was around. He was gone each morning by the time she awoke, and there were many evenings when she was already asleep before he entered their shared rooms.

When they did meet he was courteous but gave no indication that he was interested in deepening their relationship.

Denice was forced to acknowledge a yearning within her to have a real marriage with Brant once she finally admitted to herself that she loved him. She didn't know how long she had loved him but had a hunch her feelings had been there long before she married him.

Brant gave every indication that he neither wanted nor needed anything from her, particularly her love.

Denice was reminded of his attitude when she began to work with a young boy named Timothy at the hospital. Tim had never known the security of love and was distrustful of all of her overtures, yet she persisted. As Tim slowly began to respond to her, she was encouraged to hope that eventually she could gain Brant's trust and love, if she persisted.

Denice discovered many things about herself while living with Brant. Until he had entered her life, she had been unaware of herself as a woman. Now she couldn't help but notice how she reacted whenever he walked into a room; he still had the unnerving habit of silently appearing. She tried to excuse the way her heart leaped at his sudden presence, pretending that she had been startled. But Denice knew better. Even thinking about him caused a similar reaction.

Two weeks had passed since their wedding, and the tension seemed to build within her with each passing day. Something was going to have to happen. She wondered if it would help their situation if she were to open up to him and tell him how she felt. Or would it make him feel more uncomfortable? She wished she knew what to do.

Denice glanced at her watch. Brant and J.C. should be home within the hour. She went upstairs to wash up and change.

* * *

Brant absently rubbed his shoulder and tried to relax the muscles in his back and arm. He must have pulled something. Straightening in his chair, he leaned back and stared at the lights of downtown Dallas after dark. He'd seen them often since his office had been moved to the twentieth floor.

J.C. had been right. He enjoyed the challenge of his new position. His job had been made easier in some ways because J.C. had given him complete authority to make decisions. Brant had gotten into the habit of consulting with J.C. on much of it. He felt as though he'd received a crash course in the upper levels of high finance during the past two months. Only the toughest survived, and Brant knew that he was a survivor.

Yes, Brant had to admit that J.C. had read him well. Brant was in his element running the company. His confidence increased as the days went by.

He wished he felt as confident about his marriage. The situation gnawed at him because he was having a tough time dealing with his reactions whenever he was around Denice.

The truth was, he ached for her, and he hated himself for his lack of control of his emotions where she was concerned.

He would find her asleep and would stand beside the bed and savor the opportunity to enjoy her presence without having to hide how he felt. He didn't understand what it was she stirred in him.

He knew he wanted to make love to her, but it was more than that. He wanted to be around her, hear her laugh, watch her face light up with animation, wait for her elusive dimple to appear.

He caught himself thinking about her at the oddest moments—in the middle of a conference, or when he was reading a contract. Once he caught a whiff of the perfume she wore when he'd been hurrying to an appointment, and he'd stopped in his tracks, looking around for her before he was aware of what he was doing.

She haunted him, just like now. He wasn't getting any work done, sitting there thinking about Denice. Denice. His wife.

His wife. Damn. The last thing he needed was a wife, or ties of any kind. His past had taught him not to allow anyone to get close to him because it only brought pain. He didn't want to feel anything for anyone, but Denice seemed to have slipped past all of his guards, and he ached for her.

Brant suddenly stood up. Sooner or later he had to go home to the heaven and hell waiting for him. The heaven was the peace that seemed to envelop him whenever Denice was around; the hell the torment of keeping his distance from her.

Brant heard the shower running when he walked into their bedroom, and almost groaned aloud. He had been so careful to stay out of their shared quarters except when she was asleep, but his decision to come home earlier than usual had played havoc with his carefully thought out plans.

He tossed his suit coat on his bed and loosened his tie, trying to decide what to do next. The decision was removed when he heard the water stop and the shower door open. Denice had neglected to close the door to the bathroom.

"I'm home, Denice," he said in an attempt to save both of them some embarrassment.

She appeared in the doorway, her hair piled haphazardly on top of her head, strands already slipping down. A large fluffy towel covered her from chest to knees. Her smile was infectious. "Well, hello. You're early!"

"I know. I suppose I should have called first." Unconsciously he rubbed his aching shoulder.

"Don't be silly. I'm glad you're here. J.C. called earlier to say he was meeting friends for dinner."

"I know. He told me."

She looked adorable standing there in the doorway, her toes curling in the deep plush of the carpet. He cleared his throat uneasily.

"You'd better dry off before you catch cold," he offered in a low voice.

Without making a conscious decision, Denice allowed one end of the towel to drop and began to blot her skin unconcernedly. "Is something wrong with your arm? I noticed you've been rubbing it."

He abruptly turned away from the sight of her standing there before him, her skin flushed from the warm spray of water. He jerked the tie from around his neck, then realized he had a full view of her in the mirror of the dresser.

"It's nothing," he managed to mutter a little hoarsely. "I think I may have pulled a muscle."

Denice disappeared into the bathroom and came out a moment later wearing a short silk robe tied at the waist. "Would you like me to massage it for you?"

"No thanks. I'll just let the water from a hot shower work on it." He began to unbutton his shirt with fingers that had suddenly become clumsy.

She shrugged. "Suit yourself, of course." She walked into the closet, and he gave a quick sigh of relief. He made sure the bathroom door was shut before he finished undressing, ruefully acknowledging the effect her unclothed body had had on him.

It was times like this that he found himself wishing he'd ignored J.C's threats. How much was one man supposed to endure?

A marriage that wasn't a marriage. A wife that caused endless nights of lost sleep and hours of daydreaming. What sort of life was that for a man who had only sought peace and a measure of tranquillity?

Brant stood there for what seemed to be hours, trying to forget the woman in the other room, hoping the heat of the water would ease the ache in his shoulder as well as other parts of his body.

Perhaps by the time he came out she would be downstairs.

When he stepped out of the shower, he listened but heard nothing from the other room. He was relieved, since he hadn't taken the time to gather up any clothes before seeking the refuge of the bathroom earlier.

After toweling his hair, he draped the towel around his hips and entered the bedroom, where he paused just inside the doorway.

Denice had not gone downstairs. Instead, she lay curled up on the bed, asleep. A trace of tears lay on her flushed cheeks, and he winced at the sign that something was bothering her. Had she found out about J.C.'s condition?

He walked over to the bed and sat beside her, placing his hand on the small of her back.

"Denice?" he said softly. "What's wrong?"

Her long lashes fluttered, and she opened her eyes, looking confused for a moment when she saw his face so close to her own.

Hastily wiping her eyes, she rolled slightly away from him onto her back, so that his hand slid around and rested on her stomach. The thin silk of her robe did nothing to disguise the fact that she wore nothing underneath.

"Nothing's wrong."

"Why are you crying?"

"Feeling sorry for myself, I suppose," she offered in a wry tone. "The trouble with having a husband who's so self-sufficient is that I feel superfluous in your life."

He studied her for a moment, masking his surprise at her comment. The corner of his mouth lifted in a half smile. "I know the feeling," he finally replied, as though mocking himself.

Her eyes widened slightly. "That sounds strange, coming from you. You've made it obvious that you don't need anyone, nor want anyone to need you."

He tilted his head slightly, an intent expression on his face. "Is that how I appear to you?"

She forced herself to meet his level gaze when she answered him. "Yes."

"And you appear to be very organized and competent to live your own life without help from anyone."

They continued to study each other with shared wariness.

"I do need you, Brant," Denice finally admitted. "I never realized how much until I married you, but the reasons for our marriage were all wrong and I hated to admit to my feelings."

He placed his hand along her cheek, its softness causing a tingling along his palm. "I have nothing to offer you, you know."

"You have yourself, Brant. That's all any of us has."

He slowly brushed her hair along her temple and behind her ear. "You deserve so much more."

"What if you are all I want?"

The words came so softly to him that he was almost afraid he'd imagined them.

"Do you want me, Denice?"

"Very much."

He could feel the iron control he'd kept over himself slipping, his body trembling with the effort. God, he wanted her so much. She looked beautiful to him, lying there with flushed cheeks and glistening eyes. How many nights had he lain awake, imagining what it would feel like to hold her in his arms, to make love to her, to express what she made him feel?

His eyes seemed to glow with a fierce heat, and Denice felt an answering leap of desire deep within her. He might not love her, but he wanted her. It was a start.

She turned her head and placed a kiss in his palm. She heard him inhale sharply and knew her movement had surprised him. If only she knew more about lovemaking. What more could she do to encourage him?

Then his lips found hers, and she no longer wondered.
He had kissed her before, but never with so much possessiveness and heat. His tongue touched hers, then
backed away, much like a stylized dance of partners—
meeting, then parting, fencing lightly, but making their
eventual mating a promise.

Denice slid her hands up around his neck, running her
fingers through his thick hair, enjoying the silky touch
that she had often imagined.

Brant shifted on the bed, stretching his full length
alongside her, so that she was fully aligned against him.

"You feel so good," he whispered.

"So do you," she responded shyly. His towel had come
unwound from his body and she eagerly explored the
broad expanse of his shoulders and chest, the tapering
width of his waist and the firm muscles of his buttocks.
Never had she enjoyed her sense of touch more.

"You know something?" His voice was so deep she
scarcely heard him.

"What?"

"You have on too many clothes." His fingers fum-
bled at the knotted sash that secured her short robe.

Her laugh sounded ragged to her ears. "You certainly
don't seem to have that problem." She pulled away from
him slightly and loosened her sash. He pushed each side
of the robe away from her with eager hands.

"That's more like it. Now we're even."

His uneven breathing told her how much he was affected by her, and yet she knew they could never be even.
There was no way he could be as stirred by the sight of
her as she was seeing him lying there, his eyes blazing
with desire.

How could she have ever thought that Brant had no emotions? He seemed to vibrate with the intensity of his feelings, and she knew she had done the only thing possible if she wanted their relationship to work.

Like those people she had worked with who had never known love, Brant needed to be showered with unconditional responses. She could only express what she felt for him and hope that in time he would be able to respond to her.

His hands were never still. With tactile delicacy he explored her, wordlessly reassuring her by his gentleness.

Her responses were tentative and tense at first until his encouraging touch caused her to relax and enjoy what was happening.

Brant took his time, coaxing her to explore with him, willing to be the teacher and continue to learn as well. By the time he shifted his weight so that he was above her, she was clinging to him, her soft sounds of pleasure exciting him beyond measure.

His mouth took possession of hers at the same moment his body claimed hers. He felt her stiffen, and he raised his head, the tight control he held over himself evident in his face. "I don't want to hurt you," he said through tight lips.

The pressure eased somewhat, and she forced herself to exhale and relax. She had never experienced a sensation remotely like his possession of her. She knew she would never be the same now that Brant had made his claim upon her.

Brant was humbled by the expression of joy on her face as she responded. "You could never hurt me, Brant.

Never." Her eyes glistened with the moisture that beaded her long lashes. "Just love me. Please."

Slowly, then with increasing momentum, Brant set the rhythm that sent them soaring through a spectrum of sensations, each one more pleasurable than the last.

Brant felt her tense and watched her eyes fly open in surprised disbelief at what she was feeling. "Relax and let go," he whispered urgently. "Feel what I am doing to you and just let yourself go."

The words and the ragged sound of his husky voice sent her spiraling over the edge of sensation, and she cried out in surprise and pleasure.

"Oh, Brant!"

"I know, little one. I know." He allowed himself the same freedom, his body giving a convulsive lunge as he followed her into that special place and time that only lovers can experience.

Brant's body was so close to her that Denice wasn't sure whose heart thundered in her ear. Her bones seemed to have turned to mush, and she felt as though she and Brant had been melted down and poured into a mold together, their bodies still intertwined.

Brant stretched out on his side, still holding her tightly against him. She smiled sleepily, wondering if his shoulder still bothered him. Nothing seemed to have been an impediment to his lovemaking. As she drowsily rested in his possessive embrace, Denice tried to find the energy to ask him. Instead, she drifted off to sleep, enjoying his presence in her bed at last.

Ten

Cool air aroused Brant, and he reached for the covers. When his hand brushed against Denice's soft curving hip, his eyes flew open.

Light from the bathroom cast shadows in the room. He squinted at the clock and saw that it was almost midnight.

"I think we forgot to eat," Denice murmured sleepily.

"I didn't mean to wake you."

She stretched, causing her bare breasts to brush enticingly against his chest. "You didn't. My growling stomach managed to get my attention."

Brant felt more rested than he had in weeks. It felt so natural to have Denice close by his side. His hand slid along the curving contour made by her ribs, waist and hips.

"When do you suppose Morton discovered we weren't coming down to dinner?"

Denice chuckled. "I have no idea. Do you suppose if we went downstairs we'd still find him waiting patiently to serve us?"

"Somehow I doubt it. Morton strikes me as astutely intelligent. It probably didn't take him long to figure out that we had found other ways to occupy ourselves."

"Hmmm."

"What's that supposed to mean?"

"That we certainly found other ways to occupy ourselves."

Brant raised himself on one elbow and looked down at her. Their legs were still closely intertwined. "Are you sorry?"

She smiled. "Do I look as though I'm sorry?"

"I feel as though I've taken advantage of you."

"You have my permission to take advantage of me as much as you wish, and as often as you wish," she stated in her soft polished voice.

"How do you manage to make the most lewd suggestions in the most ladylike of tones?" he asked with unfeigned interest.

"All of that schooling has to show up somewhere, I suppose." She ran her fingers through the black mat of hair covering his chest. "Aren't you hungry?"

"You really are insatiable, aren't you?"

"I mean for food."

"Oh. Yes, I suppose I am. Shall we ring for room service?"

"I have a better idea. Why don't I go down and raid the pantry?"

"Why don't we both go down and see what we can find?"

Like clandestine conspirators, the two of them tiptoed down the wide staircase in their robes without turning on any lights, felt their way down the long hallway to the kitchen, made sure the door closed tightly behind them, then flipped on the light switch.

As usual, the kitchen was immaculate. The refrigerator abounded with all sorts of treats, and they piled a tray high, found a bottle of wine and two glasses, then stole up the stairway once more.

Denice burst out laughing when they reached the sanctuary of their rooms. "I can't remember ever having so much fun before. I suppose one of the drawbacks of being an only child is not having someone to share in your escapades."

Brant grinned at the picture she made—her hair tousled, her feet bare, her long length of leg stirring him with memories of recent events.

"You've got a point there." He set the tray down on a small table, and they fell upon the food like ravenous wolves, pausing occasionally to share a quip or two and to sip their wine.

Eventually Denice gave a sigh of contented repletion and leaned back in her chair. Her gaze caught a glimpse of the bed in the alcove. She glanced over at Brant.

"Would it be all right with you if I have Morton remove the other bed?"

"That all depends on where you expect me to sleep. It was my understanding I was supposed to stay close to you."

Her color heightened slightly. "I have every intention of keeping you close to me...in the same bed, as a matter of fact."

"How could I possibly mind that?"

Her expression grew serious. "Are you sorry about tonight, Brant?"

He shook his head. "Not if you aren't."

"The extra bed was my last-ditch effort at saving my pride. But I discovered that pride makes a very poor bedfellow."

"So it does. I hope you'll find me more comfortable."

She stood up and came around the table to his side. "I don't believe comfortable is quite the word I'd use to describe you." She leaned over and nibbled on his ear.

He shivered. Wrapping his arms around her, Brant pulled her into his lap. "You have others?" His mouth found the slight fluttering of her pulse at the base of her neck, and he stroked it softly with his tongue.

"I find you heart-stopping...exhilarating...intoxicating...inspiring...rousing...stimulating...breathtaking...electric—"

He began to laugh. "You're right. None of those things sound particularly comfortable to me."

Brant stood up, his arms holding Denice securely against him. "Are you ready for your second lesson?" he asked whimsically.

Denice's eyes widened involuntarily. "You mean there's more?"

"Let's just say there are some interesting variations on the central theme that can be improvised and modified as the mood strikes us." He placed her in the center of the bed, then walked into the bathroom and flipped off the light.

When he crawled into bed after removing his robe, he discovered Denice wearing nothing more than a smile. He groaned slightly as he stretched out beside her, pulling her snugly against him.

"Is your arm still hurting you?" she asked, softly stroking his shoulder.

"A little," he admitted.

"Let me see what I can do."

Before he could protest, she kneeled over him, placing her knees on each side of him, and began to knead the muscles in his chest and shoulders.

"Uh, Denice—"

"Hmmm?"

"I sincerely hope this isn't the way you normally give a massage?"

"Not normally, no."

"I'm glad to hear it."

"I try to keep my clothes on."

"You *try*? You mean you find it difficult?"

She smiled to herself at the note of outraged possessiveness that colored his voice.

"I've never found it difficult until now. Would you prefer that I put some clothes on?"

"Not on my account." He reached up and touched her breast with one hand.

"You're supposed to be relaxing."

"How can I relax with you there only inches away from me, knowing how much I enjoy touching you?"

"Try to think of me as a professional."

"I'm trying. I'm also remembering that you're my wife, and that seems to have an even stronger effect on me at the moment."

"Does your shoulder feel better?"

"Believe me, it's never felt better in my life," he said in a voice that sounded almost like a groan. "Now may I touch?"

Before she could answer, his hands came around her waist and lifted her slightly, tilting her body forward until his mouth surrounded the tip of one breast. She moaned slightly, and he paused.

"Did I hurt you?" he whispered.

"No," was her barely audible reply.

Brant rapidly resumed what he'd been doing until Denice was almost out of her mind with the pleasurable sensations he provoked within her. Still keeping her on top of him, he shifted his body until she could sheath him, joining them together once more.

Over the next several hours Brant gave Denice a comprehensive course of education into the sensuality of her own nature. She constantly amazed him with her enthusiastic and innovative responses to his lovemaking. It was as though he had awakened a part of her that neither of them had known existed, and when Brant finally fell asleep in her arms during the early hours of the morning, he recognized that Denice would always be a part of him, no matter how far he tried to go to escape.

The question was, why would he ever try?

It was almost noon the next day before Brant and Denice came downstairs. J.C. had long since finished breakfast and was working at his desk when he heard them in the hallway.

He cocked his head and listened. He heard Denice's lighter, teasing tones, and the rumble of laughter in Brant's deeper voice.

J.C. couldn't remember ever having heard that particular tone from Brant before. He sounded happy. He wondered if Brant had ever been happy. That was one of the deficiencies of a dossier. It reported everything that had ever happened to a person but couldn't report how that person had felt during it all.

He went across the hall in search of the newlyweds.

J.C. found them filling their plates at the buffet Morton had set up earlier. "Good morning," he said with a certain amount of relish.

They both glanced around at him. "Good morning," they replied in unison.

"Fine day," he offered.

They both looked at the full-length window of the dining room where rain drummed against the panes. "It is?" Denice responded doubtfully.

"Well, yes, if you don't mind spending most of your time indoors."

He caught an intimate glance exchanged between the two of them and watched with interest as Denice's color heightened slightly.

Oho! J.C. thought with glee. *The situation has definitely taken on some new aspects.* Aloud, he contented himself to casually ask, "Do you mind if I have some coffee with you two while you eat?"

"Not at all," Brant said with a relaxed smile.

J.C. noticed that they sat down next to each other at the table. It was a good thing Denice was left-handed, since it was apparent Brant was holding her right hand under the table with his left one.

"The Cowboys play the Giants at the Texas Stadium this afternoon," he announced. He waited, but received no response. "Would you two like to go with me to the game?"

Another glance was exchanged, then Brant spoke. "Another time, J.C. Denice and I have made other plans."

J.C. watched the slight confusion on Denice's face and the way her gaze was caught and held by the look in Brant's eyes. J.C. had no trouble interpreting the expression on Brant's face nor what sort of plans he had in mind. From all indications, J.C. didn't think he needed to worry about his pet project getting off the ground.

The following weeks reflected a considerable difference in the atmosphere at home and the office, and J.C. felt that at long last everything was right in his world. Even the Cowboys could do no wrong, winning every one of their games, and J.C. predicted to everyone he saw that they would win the Super Bowl that year.

J.C. particularly enjoyed the change in Brant. He seemed more relaxed. He laughed more. He seemed to have more energy than ten men, and some of his business decisions had shown a brilliant grasp of the situation, something that impressed J.C. more than he would have admitted to anyone.

Just as important, J.C. felt, was the fact that Denice seemed to be softening in her attitude toward him. Their earlier closeness was gone, and J.C. had accepted that their relationship had been changed irrevocably, but at least he hadn't lost her completely. However, it was obvious that Brant came first in her life now. J.C. couldn't lament that fact, since he was responsible for bringing them together in the first place.

His plan had worked. Even Brant and Denice would have to admit that, if he were to be tactless enough to point it out to them. There was really no need to do that, however. No need at all.

Now all J.C. had to do was to sit back and let nature take its course.

Denice couldn't remember a time in her life when she had been so happy. Brant seemed to be relaxing more and more around her and showing a loving, tender side to his nature that she found endearing in such a rugged individual.

He called her during the day whenever his busy schedule permitted for no other reason than to say he was thinking about her. He began coming home earlier evenings so that they could spend more time together.

They were on their way to Dallas for an evening's entertainment when Denice said, "You didn't need to bring me flowers tonight, you know, but they really were beautiful."

"Thank you. They reminded me of you—bright, happy-looking, shiny and new."

"Is that what I seem to you?"

He reached over and took her hand, then placed it lovingly against his thigh. He kept his hand over hers, gently stroking it. "You are everything I never expected to find in life," he admitted. "I still can't believe you're real."

She shifted her hand on his thigh and squeezed slightly. "Oh, I'm real, all right."

"Besides," he continued, "I feel that I owe you a courtship since ours was cut short by a hasty wedding."

She could feel the strong muscles beneath her fingers clench and tighten at her warm touch and smiled. "Do you mean you're courting me now?"

He nodded without glancing at her. "There are so many things I want to do for you . . . and with you. . . ." He glanced sideways and added with a wicked grin, "And to you."

Denice slid her hand a few inches up on his thigh and felt him flinch.

"If you don't quit massaging my leg, you're going to cause a wreck," he warned, and she hastily loosened her grip. He smiled and threaded her fingers through his. "Who would ever have believed that Jefferson Calhoun Roberts could ever have produced someone like you?"

"Are you still upset with him?"

"How could I be? I would have never known you if he hadn't decided to rearrange our lives for us."

"I don't think we should ever let him know. He would never let us forget the marriage was his idea."

They both laughed. Their life together was full of laughter and joy and contentment.

Brant tried not to think ahead when Denice would be faced with the loss of her parent. He hoped he would be able to fill the man's shoes when the time came. He couldn't help but wonder if anyone could.

Later that night Brant and Denice lay among their tangled sheets, mute evidence of their recent activity. No matter how often he made love to her, Brant couldn't seem to get enough of her loving warmth. He found the thought unsettling, as though he was forming an addictive habit he couldn't break. She was so responsive, so eager to join him in their love play, so willing to experience all he had to teach her.

"What are you thinking?" she asked, brushing her hand lazily across his chest.

"What makes you so sure I'm thinking about anything?"

"That little frown that forms between your brows."

"Oh."

She rubbed her fingertip across the slight ridge. "Are you going to tell me?"

"There's nothing to tell. I was just thinking about us."

"What about us?"

"What an unlikely pair we make."

"I think we make a perfectly marvelous pair, myself. We are extremely compatible."

"Maybe."

"Maybe!"

He studied her for a few moments before adding, "Or you could just be enjoying your newfound sensuality."

She raised her head and looked at him incredulously. "Do you really think I'd respond to someone else the way I do to you?"

"Maybe."

A glint of anger appeared in her eyes. "Sometimes you annoy me greatly, Mr. Malone."

"That's good to hear. For a while there I was afraid you thought I was perfect."

"Well, I wouldn't try to walk on water anytime soon, if I were you!"

He laughed.

She sat up and turned so that she was facing him. "Hasn't it ever occurred to you that the reason I respond to you so readily is because I love you?" There. After all these weeks she had finally told him.

She watched his smile fade and his face freeze into his once-familiar impassive expression. "Don't say that," he said in a low voice.

"Why not?" she managed to ask. "It's true."

"I never asked you to love me."

"I know that. The choice was mine."

"I don't want your love."

She forced herself to ignore the pain his words caused deep inside of her and tried to understand why he had said it. "Whether you want my love or not, Brant, it's yours." She watched him, but his expression didn't change. "You don't need to worry," she went on after a moment. "My love doesn't expect anything in return. It just is." She leaned over and kissed him softly on his lips. Forcing her voice to sound light and steady, she added, "Consider it as a gift—from me to you. No strings. No obligations."

He stared up at her, his expression unchanged, and she could feel her heart pounding in her chest. Then he pulled her down to him, kissing her fully, thoroughly and passionately until she no longer remembered what they had been discussing. All she knew was that she was in Brant's arms and that he wanted her. She would accept that for now because she had to. She could only pray that his love would come eventually. If not, she had enough for both of them.

Brant lay awake long after Denice had drifted off to sleep. His life had gotten more and more out of his control. The safe haven he'd made for himself over the past five years had disappeared without a trace when J. C. Roberts had stepped into his life. Nothing had been the same since.

Eventually his eyelids drifted closed, and Brant slept. But his disturbed thoughts managed to trigger a long-suppressed memory buried deep within him. Once again the dream that had haunted him for years began to unreel in his subconscious mind.

He was back in the little alleyway, the night creating a shroud of darkness around him. He saw the sagging wooden door that drunkenly hid an aging staircase. He knew the danger to him if he continued his search, but he had no choice. Trina needed him. He followed the stairs up flight after flight, hugging the wall for its dubious protection.

At last he came to the top floor. The door at the end of the hall was slightly ajar, and the familiar feeling swept over him—the sick, helpless feeling of knowing he was too late to save her.

He didn't want to go any farther, but he had to. He had to face whatever awaited him. Placing his hand on the door, he pushed slowly until it opened and he saw her—

"Brant! Wake up, Brant. You're dreaming."

Brant fought his way out of the dream state and away from the nameless terror that threatened to engulf him—to destroy him.

He opened his eyes. Moonlight spilled into the room, and by its pale light he saw Denice leaning over him.

"Are you all right?"

The past slipped away in a swirling mist once more. He ran his hands over his face and felt the dampness caused by fear and remembered pain.

"Yeah, I'm okay." He sat up in bed, his head resting in his hands.

She slid her hand across his shoulders and down his back, feeling the tensed muscles beneath her palm. "Do you dream like that often?"

He made a conscious effort to relax. "No, thank God." He forced himself to stretch out once more beside her.

Denice raised herself on one elbow, her love for him an ache deep inside. She leaned over and kissed him softly, feeling his tensed muscles slowly relax. "Is there anything I can do?"

He looked up at her concerned face, her hair tumbled around her shoulders. He touched her hair, smoothing it behind her ear. "You're already doing it. You're here." His voice was barely audible.

Remembered pain was still etched across his features, and she smoothed her fingers across the slight frown lines on his forehead.

Brant took her fingers and placed a kiss in the palm of her hand. "I'm sorry I woke you up. I used to have the same dream over and over for almost a year, but it's been several months since the last time. I thought I was over it.''

Denice tried to blank out her thoughts. She tried to re-mind herself that it was enough that it was she who was with Brant now, married to him, given the opportunity to love him. Whatever was in his past he wanted to keep there, and she needed to respect his feelings.

She tried to go back to sleep, but her brain was whirl-ing with confused thoughts. She shifted restlessly. Brant had cried out a name that even now seemed to echo in the room.

Who was Trina, and where did she belong in Brant's life?

When Brant turned over—what seemed to be hours later—Denice realized that he was as awake as she was. How could she possibly go to sleep without knowing?

''Brant?''

''Hmmm?''

''Who is Trina?''

He was silent for so long she thought he was going to ignore her question. The anguish in his voice when he had cried out the name still pierced her with its own brand of agony. She could better understand why he didn't love her if there was someone else. But where was she?

She felt him shift in bed, and she turned her head. He rearranged his pillow and propped it against the head-board, leaning back on it.

''Trina is part of my past, Denice, the part I thought I had managed to bury and forget. But life is never quite that simple. I suppose you always carry a part of that past with you. At least I have.'' He paused for a moment. ''I suppose you deserve to know more about the man you married."

He was quiet for a moment, as though gathering his thoughts, and she lay there, tense, waiting to hear whatever it was he kept so successfully hidden from the world.

"I've been on my own since I was ten years old." His voice was so low it sounded as though he were talking to himself. "I did what I had to do to survive. Jake took me in and looked after me in his own fashion until he was killed." He paused, as though once again remembering the pain of losing someone he cared about. "Then I was on my own again."

With a sudden movement, Brant pushed the covers back and stood up. The moonlight that filtered through the windows lent enough light to the room for Denice to watch his restless pacing, marveling at the muscular grace revealed by his lack of clothing.

Then once again she got caught up in his story.

"I knocked around the country, met all kinds of people and ended up being recruited by a part of our government that legally doesn't exist." He stopped his pacing and stood facing her, a silhouette in the dimly lit room.

"They trained me well. Said I was one of their best because I wasn't afraid of anything, not even dying." He sat down beside her on the bed and absently took her hand, his thoughts obviously caught up in the past. "They kept me moving, so I never stayed in one place very long. At one time or the other I lived in France, Germany, Italy, Switzerland, Belgium—I was at home anywhere and nowhere. I had no home. No family. No friends. I didn't need any."

He sat there in silence for a few moments, gripping her hand so tightly she had to bite her lip not to cry out.

"I lived that way for almost ten years. By their measurements I was successful. I didn't care what I did or where they sent me." He glanced down at her hand as though surprised to find himself holding it. He let go and stood up, walking over to the window to stare out at the night.

"Then I met Trina."

Denice heard a softness come into his voice, a tenderness that seemed to numb her heart. She waited for him to continue, determined to be strong enough to accept whatever he was willing to share with her.

"Trina was in the same line of business I was in, but for different reasons. She'd been born in East Germany. When she was eight years old, she saw her mother, father and older brother murdered. She made a vow to fight their killers any way she could." He turned away from the window and began to pace once more.

"Our childhoods were similar enough to form a bond between us. We never had much time together, our assignments often separated us, but we spent what time we could together." He paused in his pacing and looked across the room at Denice.

"Trina was the first good thing that ever happened to me. She wanted nothing from me, only to give to me. She gave everything she had—which eventually included her life." He started to pace once more.

"No one bothered to tell me about the manhunt the opposition had started to find me and take me alive. Instead, the men who directed my movements decided to use the manhunt by mounting a counteroffensive...to trap those people determined to trap me. They used Trina as the bait." His tone became agitated.

"Of course they did everything they could to protect her, and she was fully aware of her role—and made it clear that she was willing to play the part—because she loved me and wanted to help protect me." His voice reflected his pain, and Denice became aware of her silent tears trickling down her cheeks. His pain had become hers as well.

"I knew nothing about their plans. All I knew was that I hadn't heard from Trina while I was on assignment, and that worried me. We'd worked out a sophisticated form of communication that no one had stumbled across. Only she wasn't using it. I returned to Berlin earlier than anyone expected and discovered that somehow their plans had gone awry. Trina was being held as a hostage—for me." He seemed to have forgotten anyone else was in the room when he continued in a quiet tone.

"I guess I went a little wild after that. There are parts I still don't remember. Other parts I wish I could forget. When they realized they weren't going to get away, they made sure Trina didn't survive, either." He spoke of her death dispassionately. Denice bit down on her knuckle to hide the sob that seemed to fill her throat.

"There were no survivors. My boss was incensed. He said I'd cost them months of effort trying to capture and interrogate agents from the other side." As though he were talking about someone else, he added, "I almost killed him. If one of his men hadn't come to his rescue, I probably would have." He was silent for a few moments. "They found a restful place for me to stay for a few months in order to recuperate from my experience, as they called it. When I came out I had a new name, new identity, new background and a suitable job record to assist me in making it in the civilized world."

He stopped speaking and looked around the room as though he had just become aware of his surroundings and his listener.

Slowly he approached the bed, and Denice was grateful for the shadows that helped her conceal her reaction to his story.

"You wanted to know."

"Yes."

He looked around the room as though searching for something. "I need a cigarette," he finally muttered. He reached over, picked up a pair of jeans and slid into them. Then he pulled a sweater out of his drawer and jerked it over his head.

She watched his shadowy figure as he found his clothes and dressed, then walked out of the room.

The room seemed to echo with Brant's words. She could still hear the pain, the remorse, the futility. Denice felt numb, her mind and emotions incapable of registering anything more.

Because of her protected life-style, Denice had never been confronted with the reality of anything like the life Brant had lived. How did a person survive such experiences? How did he cope with his memories?

Brant's way had been to build a new life as far removed from the old one as possible. He had been content until she and her father had come into his life.

What had she and her father done to him? Of course Brant didn't love her. How could he? What did she have to offer him? Trina had understood him, had worked by his side, experienced the same dangers and excitement. Trina had known what it was like to be loved by Brant Malone.

At least now she understood him a little better, was aware that there would be parts of his life she could never understand. It was as though she had married an alien from another planet whose life-style was so different she could scarcely relate to it at all.

Yet the fact remained that Brant Malone was her husband. He had made the commitment, and she knew he intended to keep it.

As the early-morning hours slowly passed without Brant's return, Denice looked back over the past few months, remembering the first time she'd seen Brant, their first date, their wedding day.

And she remembered the first time he'd made love to her.

His past didn't matter to her. She loved the man she had come to know. She loved his gentleness and his passion. But during the long hours of the night she faced the realization that she would never experience his love.

Eleven

"What's wrong with Brant?" J.C. demanded several evenings later over dinner. He and Denice had eaten alone.

She glanced at her father. "You're the one who told me he wouldn't be home for dinner."

"I know that and that's not what I'm talking about."

"Then I don't know what you're talking about."

"He's been acting different lately—withdrawn, uncommunicative, almost surly." He cocked a brow. "Did you two have a fight?"

"Is it any of your business if we did?"

"Don't get sassy with me, young lady."

Denice carefully placed her fork on her plate and folded her hands. "Look, Father, as far as I'm concerned, you've meddled in my life for the last time. Brant and I have continued to live here with you because I knew that was what you wanted, and out of habit I've been attempting to please you. But no more. Whatever may be bothering Brant is his business—not yours, and certainly not mine."

J.C. studied his daughter for a few minutes in silence. "You've never forgiven me for asking you to marry Brant, have you?"

"For forcing me to marry him, you mean. Yes, I suppose I have. You see, I happen to love Brant Malone very much, and if you hadn't brought him home and insisted we spend time together, I would never have had the opportunity to get to know him. But no more, Father. From here on in, I will handle my life without your assistance."

"You know I love you, don't you, Denice?"

"Yes, in your own possessive way, I suppose you do. But you're going to have to let go."

"I know. I realized that when you married. I just want to see you happy."

"We all make our own happiness, Father. No one else can do that for us."

He nodded. "Do you have any plans for this evening?" he asked, in an obvious attempt to find a safer topic of conversation.

"We had tickets to the symphony. Brant may have forgotten."

"I know I'm a poor substitute, but I'd be honored to escort you in place of that handsome husband of yours."

Denice smiled. "Humility obviously rests uncomfortably upon your shoulders, Father. However, I would be pleased to have you escort me."

Much later that evening Brant sat in the study, nursing a glass of Scotch and waiting for Denice to come home. Morton had informed him that she and J.C. had gone to the symphony.

He'd forgotten their season tickets were for tonight, and he was sorry he'd missed taking her. He enjoyed listening to the symphony, which had surprised him. There were many things about his new life that surprised him, not least of which was his wife.

He didn't know what to make of her. There had never been a doubt in his mind that if she were to ever learn of his past she would be repulsed by him. So for the past several days he'd done his best to avoid being around her. Yet whenever he saw her, she treated him with the same loving affection he'd become so used to over the past few weeks.

He couldn't understand her. Nor could he understand his own feelings. He hadn't wanted to fall in love with her. In fact, he had done everything he could think of to prevent it from happening.

He didn't want to love anyone. He had learned early in life that he didn't dare love anyone. Whenever he did, something happened to them—his mother, Jake, Trina.

What he had to remember was the purpose of his marriage—to protect Denice. J.C. wouldn't always be there for her, and Brant recognized that whatever else he was feeling, he wanted to make sure that Denice was safe from harm. He at least owed her that much. She just deserved so much more.

How could he protect her from who and what he was?

Brant glanced up when the study door opened.

"Well, there you are," J.C. boomed. "How did things go this evening?"

"Just about what you'd expect." Brant glanced at Denice, then looked away. She looked like a fairy princess, standing there in her filmy dress. He fought to ignore the sudden wrenching pain that shot through him at the sight of her.

Denice walked over to Brant and bent down to kiss him. She could faintly taste the Scotch on his lips. Slowly pulling away from him, she couldn't resist allowing her fingers to touch the wave of hair that fell across his forehead.

"I'm sorry you weren't able to go tonight. I missed you."

He wanted to pull her down into the chair with him and kiss her until she made those soft little sounds that he loved to hear. His thoughts caused him to frown. "I had no choice." His voice sounded more gruff than he intended.

She forced herself to smile with a show of unconcern. "I know. Maybe next time." Walking away from him, she asked, "Have you eaten?"

"Yes."

"Would you like to join us with some coffee? Morton is preparing it."

He lifted his glass of Scotch in a parody of a toast. "No thanks."

After the few weeks of closeness, Denice felt the chasm that yawned between them with excruciating clarity. None of her education nor training had prepared her for dealing with the emotional withdrawal that Brant was obviously enacting.

She thought of the different children she had worked with. Once she had broken through their initial wall of resentment and loneliness, she'd had no trouble in getting them to accept her.

Yet she could feel Brant's rejection of her now. She wished that she understood why. Had talking about Trina brought her memory back so intensely he could no longer bear to be around his wife? Did he feel that her probing questions had finally pushed him into disclosing more about himself than he had wanted to share with anyone?

How could she know if he didn't talk to her? However, there was no way she was going to start asking any more questions. If he ever wanted to share with her, it would have to come from him.

Hours later she lay quietly beside him, listening to his even breathing as he slept. Once again, just as he had all week, Brant had stayed downstairs with J.C., giving her plenty of time to come upstairs and prepare for bed. She'd been reminded of the early days of their marriage when he'd been so aloofly polite, his dark gaze giving nothing of his thoughts away. At least now he shared a bed with her.

She turned over and curled against his back, slowly drifting off to sleep.

Sometime during the small hours of the morning, Brant came awake suddenly, then relaxed when he recognized his surroundings. His dreams had transported him to another place, another time, and it took him a moment to realize he was now in Texas, comfortably cuddled in a massive bed with his very seductive wife asleep on his shoulder.

A surge of emotion swept over him so strongly that he almost shook with it. He had tried to leave her alone, tried to go back to the way they had been at first, so that he wouldn't get confused about his role in her life.

But his mind played tricks on him, forcibly reminding him of other nights when she'd come to him so fully and passionately, so filled with love.

Love. What a deceptively simple word for such a complex emotional experience. How could he continue to fight what he felt for her? He couldn't, and it scared the hell out of him.

She felt wonderful in his arms, and he drew her closer to him, stroking her back and nuzzling her neck. Her mouth searched blindly for his, and when he returned the kiss, Brant dismissed all of his fears of the future. Instead, he allowed himself to be swayed by the intimacy of the moment.

Denice came awake to the marvelous sensations that only Brant could provoke, and she gave silent thanks that at least this part of their relationship was still necessary to him. Whatever demons he had to fight would be fought alone. She recognized that now. Somehow she had to let him know that she was there for him whenever he needed her.

Their coming together was done in silence, passion expressing itself in possessive tenderness that unconsciously healed many of their emotional wounds as it drew them even closer in their shared pain.

The next morning neither of them mentioned what had happened. Instead, they kept a casual conversation going over breakfast, and when J.C. once again invited them to accompany him to watch the Cowboys play, this time in the divisional playoffs, they agreed to go.

J.C. was relieved to see that whatever had been bothering Brant seemed to have been worked out somewhat. From the excellent view of their box seats, J.C. decided that Brant seemed more relaxed as they watched the Cowboys play one of their best games of the year. J.C. was ecstatic over the win.

When the game was over, the three of them waited for some of the crowd to clear before starting down the ramps to the car. J.C. pointed out to all who would listen that the Cowboys were destined to win the Super Bowl that year. No other team could touch them.

Brant disliked crowds. There was too much happening to watch everything and everyone. Crowds put him on edge. Instinctively he reached for Denice and pulled her close to his side, scanning the people around him out of ingrained habit.

He heard a shout and saw two security guards push through the milling crowd. Brant spun Denice around, forcing her against the concrete wall near where they stood, instinctively shielding her with his body.

Two shots rang out. People screamed. Someone was shouting, the words making no sense. Brant glanced around and froze.

J. C. Roberts lay a few feet away, a slight trickle of blood at his mouth. A much larger amount of blood welled up from a hole in his chest.

After making sure Denice was all right, Brant sprinted to J.C.'s side, checking his vital signs. The old man's eyelids flickered, then slowly opened.

"Brant?" he managed to whisper. Restlessly he moved his head.

"I'm right here, J.C."

"Denice?"

"She's fine, J.C. Just fine. Don't worry about her."

"Take care of her, son."

"You're going to be around a long time to make damn sure I do. Hang in there."

Brant was joined by a swarm of medical people, no doubt on hand for possible injuries during the game. He stepped back with a sense of helplessness and watched attendants carefully place J.C. on a stretcher to carry him down the ramp to a waiting ambulance.

He glanced around and found Denice pressed against the wall where he'd left her, her arms clutching her waist, her face a picture of horrified disbelief.

Brant walked over and slipped his arms around her. She was shaking, and he knew the cold wind sweeping over the stadium wasn't helping her shocked condition.

"Come on, love," he murmured. "Let's get to the car."

"He's dead, isn't he?" she whispered.

Brant fought to keep all emotion out of his voice. "J.C.'s too tough to die. You know that. Come on, let's get to the hospital."

Denice couldn't seem to get her legs to work. She tried to take a step, but she only managed to sway. Brant swept her up in his arms and strode down the ramp to the car and Harris. He gave the anxious chauffeur a brief description of what had happened while he climbed into the back with Denice still in his arms.

"Who shot him?" Denice finally found the words to ask.

"I don't know. But I sure as hell intend to find out." He sat with his arms around her as Harris managed to get through the thinning crowd in record time, heading for the hospital. They could hear the wailing sound of the ambulance siren in the distance.

Once again Brant's life seemed to be filled with violence, terror, blood and pain. But this time it was going to be different. He had a family now, and he wasn't going to allow some bastard to destroy it, not if he could help it.

How ironic it would be if the condition that had caused Brant to marry J.C.'s daughter didn't kill him after all. Instead, an unknown assailant's attack could cause the same end result.

For the first time since he was a child, Brant found himself praying.

Denice sat in a small lounge near the surgical ward of the hospital, waiting for word about her father. She heard brisk footsteps along the hallway and looked up expectantly.

Brant walked in, and she came to her feet. He shook his head. "I haven't heard anything, have you?"

"No, not since they took him into surgery." They walked over to a small sofa and sat down. "What did the police say?"

"They have the man in custody, but he's not giving them any information. No motive, nothing. From the looks of things, he may have been hired for the job."

"What are the police going to do?"

"Find out who hired him." He walked over to the window and glanced through the blinds. "So am I."

The quiet intensity of his voice caused a shiver to go through Denice. "What do you mean?"

Brant walked back to where Denice stood. "Your father knew what kind of man he wanted to protect you. Well, he's going to get his money's worth. I'm going to find the man who caused this." He spoke in a soft, quiet voice, but Denice recognized the determined vow.

"Brant—"

"I know you don't approve of who and what I am, Denice, but you're not going to stop me."

She watched the man she loved for a moment, feeling his pain as well as her own. "You love Father, too, don't you?"

"Love? I don't know much about it. But I respect J.C. He didn't deserve this."

Tears began to pour down her cheeks once more. "I don't want him to die."

Brant pulled her close into his arms. "I know, love. But whatever happens, you know I'm here for you." He could feel her agony as though it were his own, and perhaps it was. They stood there in the middle of the hospital waiting room, drawing comfort from each other and trying not to think about the possibilities ahead.

Denice raised her head from Brant's shoulder at the sound of someone walking into the room. "Harry!" She walked over to Dr. Fairchild and hugged him.

"I came as soon as I heard."

"Have you seen him?"

"No. He's still in surgery. But he's got the best surgeon there is working on him. If anybody can pull him through, it will be Perlman." He looked past Denice to Brant. "Sorry our next meeting after the wedding had to be under these circumstances. This isn't much of a honeymoon for you two."

Brant shook the doctor's hand. "At the moment our only concern is J.C. What do you think?"

Harry shook his head. "According to the medical report, it doesn't look too good. He's lost a lot of blood, and his age is against him."

Brant glanced at Denice. She might as well be prepared for the worst. Turning back to the doctor, he asked, "How is this going to affect his other condition?"

Harry looked confused. "What other condition?"

"You don't have to hide it from me, Dr. Fairchild. J.C. told me last fall that you gave him only a few months to live—possibly to the new year."

Denice gave a little cry and sank down in a chair.

"J.C. told you that?" Harry asked incredulously.

"Yes."

"That son of a— The man should be horsewhipped."

"What are you talking about?"

"Until he became intimate with a bullet, J. C. Roberts's only health problem was shedding some of that weight, which he agreed to do. Considering the fact he didn't take proper care of himself, J.C. was in reasonably good health. I certainly never gave him any such prognosis."

Brant stared at the smaller man before him, trying to assimilate this new piece of information. J.C. had lied to him. Again. He began to smile. He really was a bastard. Every time he was caught in a lie, he told a bigger one.

Brant began to chuckle. The man was something else. Somehow he had known how to appeal to Brant's protective instincts. He had come up with a lie that would appeal to Brant's need to look after Denice. What a Machiavellian mind the man possessed.

"Why would J.C. make up such a tale?" Dr. Fairchild asked.

"There's no telling," Brant finally responded, shaking his head, leaving his private opinion of J.C.'s motives to himself.

"Well, it was a hell of a thing for him to say. It's almost as though the man were predicting his own end." Harry shook his head. "He's a hard one to understand."

"Impossible is a better word," Brant suggested. He looked over at Denice, who still seemed to be in a state of shock. "Would you like some coffee?"

She nodded, staring up at him with a bewildered expression.

"I'll go find us some. I'll see you two later." Brant disappeared down the hallway.

Harry sat down beside Denice. "J.C.'s a tough old bird, honey. He's got a lot of fight in him. He won't let something like this get him down."

All Denice could think about at the moment was the look on Brant's face when he'd discovered that J.C. had lied to him. Was that how he'd gotten Brant to marry her?

If so, it had worked. The lie had worked. And now J.C. might discover that his tall tale had become prophetic.

Brant had returned with the coffee by the time the surgeon came to talk with them.

"He came through surgery all right and is in stable condition," Dr. Perlman informed them, "but he's still on the critical list. The bullet went through his lung and caused considerable damage. I can't predict what may happen from here. I did all I could."

"I know you did, Dr. Perlman," Denice responded. "Thank you."

"We're going to keep him in recovery until morning. Then he'll be in intensive care where visiting is limited. I would suggest you go home and get some rest. We'll call you if there's any change."

Brant led Denice down the hallway to the elevator. When they reached the lobby, they walked outside where Harris waited. Brant was forcibly reminded that none of J.C.'s money would help him now.

He placed Denice in the car. "You go on home and get some rest. I'll see you later."

She looked at him in surprise. "But what about you? Where are you going?"

"I've got some things to check out."

"Brant, don't do anything...foolish, please," she pleaded.

"Don't worry about me. Try to get some rest."

He started to close the door.

"Brant?"

He paused and looked down at her. She placed her hand on his cheek. "I love you so much. I couldn't bear it if I were to lose both of you."

Her words and gesture caught him off guard, and he stood there, frozen in place. "You still love me?" he questioned softly, disbelief obvious in his tone.

"Still? I never stopped loving you, Brant. I never will."

He leaned over and kissed her briefly—a hard, possessive kiss like none she'd ever received from him before. "Don't worry. You aren't going to lose me, love. I've got too much to live for."

He straightened, closed the door and watched as the car pulled down the long driveway. Then he glanced at his watch. He was going to need some help on this one, and he knew just whom to call. Brant Malone was going to start calling in favors, starting right now.

Twelve

———

Denice woke up suddenly, sensing movement in the room. "Brant?"

"Yes, love. I didn't mean to wake you." He slid into bed next to her and hungrily reached for her. "Have you heard any more from the hospital?"

"No. I called when I got home, but there was no change."

"He's going to be all right. I know he is."

"Brant?"

"What is it?"

"Where have you been?"

"Working."

"At the office?"

"Some of the time."

"How did you get home?"

"Rented a car. Why don't you try to get some sleep?"

"I'm scared, Brant."

"About what?"

"Everything. The shooting, the threats, what's happening in our lives."

"The shooting was engineered by the same person who's been sending the threats."

She pulled away from him in surprise. "You mean you found out who it is?"

"I have a fairly good idea. Your father's investigative team had quite an interesting accumulation of information that they shared with me after a little persuasion. I don't think there's going to be anything to be scared about. He won't hurt you, I'll guarantee that."

"Who is he?"

"The son of a former partner of J.C.'s. According to the reports, he's made statements to the effect that J.C. caused his father to fail in business, that he stole from him, that he even caused the heart attack that killed his father."

"How could that be true?"

"It probably isn't. And even if it is true, you don't go around trying to kill people because of it."

Denice snuggled closer to Brant. "I'm so glad you're here. I missed you."

"I missed you, too. That's why I came tonight...to let you know I'm going to have to go out of town for a few days, and I didn't want to leave without saying goodbye."

"Why now?"

"It's part of the investigation. The man implicated in the shooting lives back East."

"What are you going to do?"

"Whatever it takes."

"Oh, Brant."

"J.C. wanted me around for protection. Unfortunately, I was unable to protect him quite enough, but I won't slip up again."

"Father convinced you he was dying, didn't he? That's why you agreed to marry me, isn't it?"

Brant kissed her, a soft, lingering kiss that caused her to forget her questions. When he paused for a breath, he said, "I married you because I wanted to marry you, Denice."

"That isn't what you said at first."

"I lied."

"Something else you and Father seem to have in common."

He chuckled. "Good point. Your father has always said he and I were a lot alike."

"I'm sorry about all my questions, and especially sorry for asking about Trina. You had the right to your own privacy. I didn't mean to remind you of your pain."

Brant lay there in silence, and Denice wished she could cut her tongue out. Why had she brought up such a painful subject at this time?

"That was the first time I'd ever talked about what happened, and I discovered that it helped. By facing what had happened, I began to see that I could let go of it and let it stay in the past where it belonged." He kissed her just below her ear. "You really helped me to do that, so you don't owe me any apologies."

"I know I can never replace Trina in your life, but I would like for us to build a relationship on mutual trust and respect. Will that be enough for you, Brant?"

"Will it be enough for you?"

"Yes, of course."

"You don't want my love?"

"Brant, I'll never ask more of you than you're willing to give to me."

"And if I want to give my love to you, will you accept it?"

She tried to see his face in the shadowy room, convinced she had misunderstood. "Brant?" she whispered breathlessly.

"This week has taught me quite a bit about myself and how I've been fooling myself about my feelings for you, for J.C., and my past." He began to stroke his hand up and down her spine, enjoying the feel of her warm body pressed so closely against him. "Today all of those feelings crystallized for me. I don't know why by refusing to acknowledge my feelings for you I thought they might go away." He smiled down at her. "They haven't, you know."

"Oh, Brant, I love you so much."

"I love you, too, Denice, more than I can possibly show you. Having you in my life has taught me so much about love and what it can do to change a person, to heal old hurts and get rid of pain."

Tears slipped down her cheeks once again. Never had she cried so much in one day, but these tears were of joy. No matter how much love she had to give, there always seemed to be more.

She clung to him, and he held her close in his arms, warming her, soothing her, and by his very presence reassuring her that he was a part of her life.

But when she woke up the next morning, he was gone.

For the next several days Denice spent most of her time at the hospital with J.C. There were times when she was afraid they were going to lose him, but J.C.'s indomitable will to live kept him going until he finally seemed to be on the mend.

He asked for Brant, and she had to explain that Brant wasn't there. She hadn't seen him nor heard from him since the night J.C. had been shot. It was as though he had disappeared, stepped into another dimension, where she was unable to follow.

Denice tried to imagine her life without Brant, tried to recall how she'd spent her days and nights before he'd become such a vital part of her existence. Had she really led such a sterile life—with so little joy, laughter and love?

As the days passed with no word from Brant, she began to wonder if she'd ever see him again. Where had he gone? When would he return? And if he didn't, where would she get the strength to face the future without him?

J.C.'s recovery was slow. Denice spent most of her days and evenings with him. His weakness forcibly reminded her of how close she had come to losing him. Whatever his faults, J.C. was her father, and she loved him very much.

She found herself frequently praying for the safety of both of the men in her life.

The constant, burning pain in his chest caused J.C. to stir in his sleep. His eyes slowly opened, and he vaguely noted the darkness and the quiet of late night at the hospital. His night-light cast a soft glow in the room, creating familiar shadows.

Restlessly turning his head, his eye caught an unaccustomed shadow. He looked toward the chair next to his bed and saw Brant sitting there, quietly watching him.

"What are you doing here?" J.C. asked in a gruff whisper.

"Checking up on you."

"How did you get past the watchdogs on duty out there?" He nodded toward the door.

"Experience," Brant said with a slight smile.

J.C. started to laugh, then held his bandaged chest in protest of the sudden movement. "I've missed you, boy. Where've you been?"

"Tracking down the man who put you in here."

J.C. nodded. "I figured as much. Have you seen Denice?"

"Not yet."

"She misses you."

"I know the feeling."

The two men studied each other for a moment in silence. J.C. smiled slightly, satisfied with what he read on Brant's face.

"What did you find out?"

"Does the name Travis Benton mean anything to you?"

"Benton?" J.C. lay quietly for a moment. "Any kin to Montgomery Benton?"

"His son."

"He's behind this?"

"And the threatening notes. Why didn't you tell me what was going on, J.C.? It would have made my job a hell of a lot easier."

"Thought I could handle it myself. Must be getting old."

Brant watched the older man in silence. Without conscious thought, he reached over and touched J.C.'s hand, which still lay on his chest.

"You did all right. Once I got the information your investigators had been gathering so meticulously, I was able to move in." He straightened in his chair slightly. "Mr. Benton is no longer a threat."

J.C.'s hooded eyes widened slightly. "Is he dead?"

Brant's chuckle lightened the suddenly tense atmosphere of the room. "No, J.C. The man is very much alive. Did you think I'd kill him?" he stated, amusement apparent in his voice.

"Of course not," J.C. muttered.

"I just assisted the authorities with their investigation. As a matter of fact, they were quite appreciative of my efforts. Even offered me a job."

J.C. eyed the younger man sternly. "You already have a job."

"You're telling me. Keeping you out of mischief looks to be a full-time occupation." The affection in his voice caused a lump to form in J.C.'s throat.

"Thanks for coming in tonight. I'll be able to rest easier, knowing you're back home," J.C. admitted.

J.C.'s words, as well as the gruffness in his voice, grabbed at Brant's emotions. He gave a gentle squeeze to J.C.'s hand. "I'm glad to *be* home." Once again the men

exchanged a wordless message before Brant turned and
silently left the room.

Denice's dream seemed so real. Once again she was in
Brant's arms. He held her close, so close she could feel his
warm, muscular body pressed against her.

"Oh, Brant," she murmured, her hands lovingly ca-
ressing his back.

"Did you miss me?" he whispered, kissing her softly.

Her eyes flew open. Dreams didn't talk. She found
herself securely locked in Brant's arms. "You're home!"
she whispered breathlessly.

"Do you mean you just now discovered that fact?" He
deliberately moved his thigh, which was intimately tucked
between hers. "Do you respond this way to every man
who crawls into your bed?"

She began to place tiny kisses along his jaw and cheek.
"Absolutely," she agreed with unfeigned enthusiasm.

He laughed—a relaxed, free sound that caused her
heart to pound with anticipation and love. "Good thing
we have a damned efficient security system around here.
A poor burglar wouldn't know what hit him."

"Are you all right?" she asked, running her hands over
him as though searching for wounds.

"I've never been better." His hands were far from idle
as he reacquainted himself with Denice's soft and seductive body.

"J.C.'s doing remarkably well, considering everything."

"I know. I stopped by to check on him."

"Did you find the man responsible for the shooting?"

"Yes. His hired gun was only too glad to fill in the necessary details to convict him."

Denice gave a sigh of relief. "Then it's finally over."

Brant kissed her—a slow, searching, inquisitive kiss. When he paused, his breathing erratic, he concurred, "Yes, some things are over." Then his voice dropped to a gruff whisper. "Other things are just beginning."

With leisurely movements Brant touched and caressed her, wordlessly admitting how much he had missed her. Denice's loving response convinced him that he had, indeed, come home.

J.C.'s homecoming became a cause for celebration. He'd gotten a clean bill of health from the doctor and looked healthy and well rested.

"It's about damned time they let me out of there," he grumbled over dinner his first evening at home.

"Don't kid us, Father. You adored all the attention."

"The hell I did. Damned nurses coming in and out, sticking things into me, waking me up to take a damned sleeping pill, coming in before dawn to do unspeakable things to my body."

"At least the Cowboys came through at the Super Bowl this year," Brant pointed out. "That should count for something."

"Except I had to watch the game on television."

"I swear, J.C.," Brant remarked, trying not to smile, "you'd probably complain if you were being hung with a new rope. I've never heard so much complaining."

J.C. raised his brows. "It's my home. I can complain if I feel like it."

Brant and Denice exchanged amused glances. "You have a point, Father," Denice agreed.

He leaned slightly forward in his chair and frowned at his daughter. "What I want to know from you is, have you started on my grandchildren yet?"

"Father!" His sudden change of subject and the surprising subject matter caught her totally unprepared.

Brant began to laugh. "I always knew I got lied to and blackmailed in order to provide stud service for this family. At least now you're getting around to admitting it."

"I'm not admitting a thing!"

"Come on, J.C. Harry told me there wasn't a thing wrong with your health last fall when you played out that sad scene about not lasting to the new year. What the hell was that all about?"

J.C. leaned back in his chair and surveyed his son-in-law from behind lowered eyelids. "I'm sure as hell not getting any younger. If I'd waited for Denice to think about providing me with grandbabies, I would have never lived to see them."

In a more sober voice, Brant said, "You're lucky to be alive today, and you know it."

"I agree."

"Do you also agree that you didn't need me here guarding Denice any more than you needed me down at the office running the business?"

"The hell I didn't! I'm too old to put in the hours necessary to keep up with everything. I need you to take over and let me rest."

Brant winked at Denice. "I didn't have to marry your daughter in order to run the business."

"It works out better this way. Much more tidy."

Brant shook his head. "Well, J.C., since I know to what extent you went to arrange our marriage, and now that you've finally admitted why you considered it necessary, I suppose I'd better excuse myself and start earning my keep."

J.C. glanced at him suspiciously. "What do you mean?"

"I think Denice and I will retire early tonight. You ask a lot of a man, both at the office and at home, but I've never been one to shirk my duties." His bland expression could not hide the amusement in his eyes when he held out his hand to Denice. "Ready, love?"

She bit her lip, determined not to laugh at the look on her father's face. She stood up and smiled at Brant. "Yes, as a matter of fact, I am." She turned to J.C. "It's also time for you to get back to bed. There's no sense in overdoing it on your first day home."

She and Brant watched as Morton assisted J.C. to his room, then went to their own apartment. They waited until they reached the bedroom before bursting into laughter.

After stripping off their clothes, Brant and Denice went into the bathroom and crawled into the Jacuzzi that awaited them. As soon as Brant sat down in the water, she crawled into his lap, facing him.

"Don't you think you were a little hard on Father tonight?" she asked, kissing the tip of his nose.

"Sorry, love. I couldn't resist. He's so damned pleased with himself these days. I swear he thinks the term 'father knows best' refers to him."

He put his hands around her back and began to slowly stroke up and down from her neck to her hips.

"Hmmm, that feels good."

"Maybe you should teach me how to give a massage."

"Great idea. With your hands you'd be marvelous."

After a few minutes of silence, Denice tentatively said, "You know, we've never talked about a family."

"I know."

"Don't you want one?"

"I never thought I could have one. Don't you understand yet? I figured that, once a woman knew about me and my past, she'd go running into the night, screaming to get away from me. I never thought I'd be given the chance to have a family."

"Did you think I was going to do that after you told me?"

"There was a damned good possibility, yes. But you're so honorable, I knew you'd probably stick to your commitment, regardless of how you felt personally."

"Brant, don't you understand yet that I don't care what you used to do, the kind of person you were? None of that matters to me. It's who you are today that's important. I love the man you are, and I very much hope that I can have your children someday."

"You really want a family?" he asked.

"If they will all look like you."

"Heaven forbid."

"The question is, what do you want?"

"I want to be able to live with you and love you for the rest of my life."

"That's what I want, too," she whispered.

"See how easy it is to fulfill my needs?"

"Do you want to stay here with Father or live somewhere else?"

"That's up to you."

"He'd really be lonesome if we left."

"I'm sure of it."

"I think he'd like to be around our family when we have one."

"You've answered your own question, then." Brant pulled her closer, enjoying the touch of her bare breasts against his chest.

He began to nibble along her jawline, tasting her, enjoying having her to himself for a while.

She leaned back in his arms and looked at him, her face serious. "Are you angry with Father for putting us through all of this for no other reason than because he wants grandchildren?"

"Do I look angry?" She shook her head. "Am I acting angry?" She shook her head. He gave her a lingering, very thorough kiss. "Do I feel angry?" he whispered.

"I'm not sure. Maybe you should try that one more time."

Brant picked her up and carried her, dripping, into the bedroom. "Better than that, I'll give a full-scale demonstration."

Epilogue

———

"Grampa, Grampa, come see what I made!" Three-year-old Kristina danced into the study where J.C. sat reading. He looked over his glasses and smiled. Holding out his arms, he wordlessly invited his young visitor onto his lap.

She needed no second invitation.

"Well, Krissie, tell Grampa what you made."

"A house and a fence and a barn and—"

"Did you draw them?"

"Uh-uh. I made them with my blocks. Come see."

He scooped her up in his arms and stood up. "By all means, we must see this masterpiece. If my granddaughter has decided to become an architect—"

"You're going to rush out and buy her a firm of architects to play with, no doubt," Brant finished for him.

J.C. grinned. "That's a thought. What are *you* doing here?"

Brant raised an eyebrow and smiled at the older man. "I live here, or have you forgotten?" he asked, setting down his briefcase on a nearby table.

"How could I forget with all this evidence racing around the place?" He nodded at the little girl in his arms, her black curls drawn up in clusters over each ear.

Brant sat down and stretched out in a chair with a sigh of contentment. "Wasn't that what you bought me for?" he asked in a lazy drawl.

"Bought you! Dammit, Brant, I wish you'd quit talking that way. It's been four years now and... admit it. You and Denice couldn't be happier!"

Brant cocked his head slightly. "I suppose you're taking credit for that?"

"I introduced you, didn't I? I knew as soon as I met you the two of you were meant for each other."

Kristina wriggled down from her grandfather's arms and trotted over to her daddy. Crawling into his lap, she threw her arms around his neck and gave him a loud kiss on the cheek. In return she got a hug and a kiss that caused her to giggle with satisfaction.

Brant looked over at J.C. and shook his head. "I'm afraid you didn't fit my image of Cupid, J.C."

Denice walked into the room carrying nine-month-old Michael. "Hello, darling. Glad to see you made it home on time."

"On time for what?" J.C. asked.

Michael reached for his daddy when Denice leaned over to kiss Brant. He took the second child and cuddled him against his chest.

"We've got tickets for a new musical," Denice explained. "So we're planning a night out on the town—dinner, the theater, the whole works."

"Humph. I suppose you expect me to baby-sit." J.C. tried not to show his eagerness.

"Wouldn't think of it, Father. That's why we hired Nora."

"I could probably tell them a story or two."

Brant spoke up. "I can just imagine the sort of story you'd tell them."

J.C. looked affronted. "I am very good with stories, aren't I, Krissie?"

She nodded her head where she lay against Brant's shoulder. Denice smiled at the picture Brant made, a child in each arm, his contented expression filling her with a feeling of joy.

"May I get you a drink?" she asked him when he noticed her watching him.

He shook his head. "No. I really don't need it anymore. I get enough stimulation without it." He began to laugh at the look she gave him. "You might check with Cupid over there. He looks as though he could use one."

"Cupid?" She glanced around at J.C., puzzled.

"I still say that you both owe me your gratitude. Without me you wouldn't have found the happiness you share, you wouldn't have those two beautiful children, and you certainly wouldn't be enjoying a marriage that was obviously made in heaven."

J.C. couldn't understand what he had said to cause Brant and Denice to burst out laughing.

 **Silhouette Desire**

COMING NEXT MONTH

THERE ONCE WAS A LOVER—Dixie Browning
There once was a woman named Jo, who found she could never say no. Her love for Clay Abbott was more than a habit, she discovered he'd never let go!

FORBIDDEN FANTASIES—Gina Caimi
Was Ava's marriage a legend come to life? While filming a medieval love story of passion and betrayal, Ava found her own husband was the star of her wildest fantasies.

THEN CAME LOVE—Nancy Gramm
Maggie was determined to have a child, and Sam was exactly what she wanted in father material—for only one night. But with Sam, one night would never be enough.

JUST JOE—Marley Morgan
Quarterback Joe Ryan was the stuff women's dreams were made of . . . and he knew he could soothe Mattie's nightmares. But could he be her sweetest dream come true?

STOLEN DAY—Lass Small
A magical country fair brought Priscilla and Quinlan together. Quinlan insisted that she was the keeper of his quest and that his love would last a lifetime past their stolen day.

THE CHALLONER BRIDE—Stephanie James
Angie was destined to have a part in creating Flynn Challoner's empire, but she refused to marry for less than love . . . so why did she find herself dreaming of becoming a Challoner bride?

AVAILABLE NOW:

WHAT THIS PASSION MEANS
Ann Major

THE SOUND OF GOODBYE
BJ James

A FRAGILE BEAUTY
Lucy Gordon

THE SKY'S THE LIMIT
Syrie A. Astrahan

GAME, SET, MATCH
Ariel Berk

MADE IN HEAVEN
Annette Broadrick